THE LONG SUIT

PHILIP DAVISON

PENGUIN BOOKS

PENGUIN BOOKS

Published by the Penguin Group
Penguin Group (USA) Inc., 375 Hudson Street,
New York, New York 10014, U.S.A.
Penguin Books Ltd, 80 Strand, London WC2R 0RL, England
Penguin Books Australia Ltd, 250 Camberwell Road,
Camberwell, Victoria 3124, Australia
Penguin Books Canada Ltd, 10 Alcorn Avenue, Toronto,
Ontario, Canada M4V 3B2
Penguin Books India (P) Ltd, 11 Community Centre,
Panchsheel Park, New Delhi – 110 017, India
Penguin Books (N.Z.) Ltd, Cnr Rosedale and Airborne Roads,
Albany, Auckland, New Zealand
Penguin Books (South Africa) (Pty) Ltd, 24 Sturdee Avenue,
Rosebank, Johannesburg 2196, South Africa

Penguin Books Ltd, Registered Offices:
80 Strand, London WC2R 0RL, England

First published in Great Britain by Jonathan Cape 2003
Published in Penguin Books 2004

1 3 5 7 9 10 8 6 4 2

LIBRARY OF CONGRESS CATALOGING IN PUBLICATION DATA
Davison, Philip, 1957–
The long suit / Philip Davison.
p. cm.
ISBN 0 14 20.0199 6
1 British—New York (State)—Fiction.   2. Intelligence officers—Fiction.
3. Long Island (N.Y.)—Fiction.   I. Title.
PR6054.A896L66 2004
823'.914—dc22   2003066043

Printed in the United States of America

For Alison
with her light

Grateful thanks to my editor, Robin Robertson;
also to Jonathan Sissons and Tristan Jones

What of the night?

    The watchman said, The morning cometh, and also the night.

ISAIAH, 21:11–12

LONG SUIT A thing at which one excels.

The Concise Oxford Dictionary

Chapter 1

I had my own troubles, some of which I had addressed. When they lifted me my plan had been to go to ground, let time pass and be vigilant. Like a Druid, I had come to count nights instead of days.

I watched Clements talking to somebody at the end of the corridor. He was loud, but I couldn't make out the words. The lower jaw seemed to have just the one spring action. He was like a thirsty dog drinking from a water pistol.

I knew that he was fully aware of my presence. When he came my way it was clear he was going to pass and ignore me, so I stood up to present myself. He was a bad judge of human movement – that was another of his animal traits. He lurched past with exaggerated politeness.

Another new start, and against my better judgement. A new start in the same murky pool from which I thought I had finally escaped. I knew from the outset that something was not right. I had seen this clumsy civil servant act before. All my fears are old fears.

When Clements entered an office further down the corridor and left the door open I knew that my name had not been struck off the unwritten list of bob-a-job men, known among these people as understrappers. Not that you are ever formally given the title. Nor are you aware that you are going to be made an understrapper. You are altogether more ambitious.

To get you started some snivelling little minion meets you in some dive at an inconvenient time, gives you a verbal brief and a few quid up front. He'll tell you that usually the payment for the first job comes in the form of bank notes torn in half – you get the second half when the job is done. But he likes you, he tells you. He thinks you can be trusted, so he gives you a proper advance.

Another myth he'll sell you is that your breaking into a solicitor's office or your money-laundering activities or your unofficial surveillance work is special rather than routine, and that a good understrapper lives like the animals that occupy the tree canopy and rarely walk the earth.

As a rule, you don't get invited to walk down these corridors. I looked at the open door. They must have something special planned for me, I thought.

I waited to be called. There was no immediate summons. This was one of two offices. Clements had another in Whitehall.

There might be some hand-wringing, I thought, behaving like a monk with his mistress. That would be part of the act. What unsavoury thing would he drag out into the light?

Eventually, a thin, handsome man by the name of Jack Bradley stuck his head around the door frame. He was wearing a tailored suit which had been made for him a long time ago, and a pair of shoes that had been stitched by a gorilla. 'Right,' he said. He gave me a round of his novelty cough, which was a rasp spliced to an owl hoot. He had arranged the meeting.

It was interesting that the cough was not a polite interruption, but came after he had spoken. It was a conspicuous assertion of a hard-pressed professional's busy schedule.

I didn't like his tone, the forced freshness. There are Bradley's kind in most organisations. Fiercely ambitious people stuck in middle management. They compete at all levels. They compete for parking spaces.

Let me make it absolutely clear – I didn't like Bradley, and there were other reasons.

I rose to my feet and followed Bradley through the open door. There were hard chairs on the near side of the desk, and one easy chair against the wall. Clements was sitting on a hard chair behind the desk that wasn't part of the set. He was very proud of his self-assembly reproduction Bodleian chair. It was made of English elm, had a broad, contoured seat and a cage back. He had bought the kit in Oxford and assembled it in his garage in Richmond. Bradley had already briefed me on the importance of the chair and the vanity it had come to represent. It was one of those casual intimacies that came your way in the firm from time to time. The kind of gossip those who prided themselves on being realists liked to trade.

'I see you like this chair,' Clements said.

It was a leading remark. No, I didn't like it, but nor did I dislike it.

'I put it together myself.'

I got a little charge of satisfaction from having

intelligence about the man's chair, but quickly decided that Clements probably did this sort of thing all the time; that is to say, he knew Bradley told everybody about the chair. I had to play along.

'You did? That must give you genuine satisfaction.'

'It does,' he said, going into a slouch. He was on to me immediately. A little chill crept into his tone.

'Four hundred and ninety-five quid, it cost,' Bradley had told me. He didn't know whether or not that included the glue.

'You're a practical chap, I hear.'

'No good with the D.I.Y., but otherwise . . .'

To be fair to him, it wasn't a bad effort. The chair was probably quite comfortable to sit in and would last. I just didn't want to get cozy with Clements, or Bradley for that matter.

Clements turned away to gaze out of the window into the fog, affecting a sudden lack of interest. Bradley stood with a hunch that made me think the coat-hanger was still in his jacket.

It had been nice moving through the city in the fog. I had imagined aeroplanes taxiing along the streets. People getting to places they had to be.

Clements was being inscrutable. There was a popular notion in the firm that if you stayed around long enough you'd go simple, but, given the nature of the job, who would be able to identify the simpletons? Age wasn't always a reliable measure.

Bradley indicated that I should sit. He was going to stand. He was going to force the pace.

Upper management like his sort. They can rely on their ruthlessness. They know that these people will not allow professional or personal relationships to impede their work. They get frustrated with lack of promotion, but simply try harder. Occasionally, they explode and somebody has to go after them with a net. Ask Clements about the Bradleys of this world and he will tell you they are created, not born, and therefore are prone to stalling.

'We know all about you, Harry,' Bradley said. His innocent act was different from that of Clements. It was laced with a variable knowingness that purportedly stretched back into the mists of time.

'You must be very tired from doing your homework, Mr Bradley,' I replied. Clements turned from the window with a grimace fixed on his face. I thought he was going to say something about the fog.

'We know what you've been up to,' he said, looking to Bradley. 'Isn't that what you mean, Jack?' If I had dinner in Mr Clements's house I would get an apple for dessert.

Bradley knew he didn't need to reply directly. 'I told my Chaps not to bother you until you were finished with what you were at. They didn't bother you, did they?' Chaps are vicious public school twits with pensionable jobs. The security mob. One of these monkeys had used Bradley's phrase: he had told me that he knew all about me.

I looked about the room. There was a clutter of heavy furniture surrounding the hard chairs. It was an animal den full of obstacles that doubled as hides and perches.

If these men didn't get what they wanted they would soon be leaping from one lump to another, all the while carrying on with the same corporate coyness.

My tongue was thick. My hands were cold. I didn't belong here. None of us belonged. That was the way it worked.

Misfits together. None of us belonging.

'We know about the killing,' Clements said.

'Call a policeman.' I said.

'You disappear without telling us and then you do this.'

'Not good on procedure?' Bradley chimed in.

'Harry, you can't be doing this sort of thing,' said Clements mildly. 'Bad news. Bad for everybody.'

'Sorry.'

I gave him the set jaw. The fixed gaze. I was trying to remember every detail when I should have been concentrating solely on what was important.

'You had good reason, I'm sure,' continued Clements, 'but was it protecting life and limb, we ask? We're a bit hazy on that one.'

Bradley leaned over towards me. 'Protecting the innocent,' he echoed, with an encouraging nod of his head. 'That's what I've been telling Mr Clements. Harry's a good man.'

Clements wet his lips and gave Bradley an indulgent look. I could tell Clements was happy sending memos reprimanding the dead. 'No doubt,' he said.

'We just might have something for you,' Bradley continued.

'I don't want any trouble,' I said.

'Of course you don't, Harry,' Clements boomed merrily. 'You're a killer.'

'It was me who told Mr Clements you're a killer,' Bradley added helpfully.

They were both still managing to sound coy. My head began to fill with black mud. Now I had to play games. I had to pretend this utterance was a compliment and, accordingly, I responded with a lolling of my head.

I was told that there was a situation developing. That was the description. It doesn't get more vague than that.

I could have run earlier but I hadn't. There must come a moment when you say no to this. Had it just passed? Was it here and now?

There was more sinister flattery. More lolling of the head. Had they told me a lot of sky was needed to build an airport I would have made the same lolling motions.

I should have spoken up. I should have told them that my day had been run through with small reversals. A recurrent thought telegraphed that if I could just speak in the right key they would accept that I was the wrong man for the job. I would settle for something more menial. I wanted to be an understrapper again.

I left the building and turned my face to the fresh breeze that was coming up the river. I felt their eyes on my back. That was normal, of course. How could it be any other way?

As I began to walk I was conscious of shading my misgivings from those penetrating eyes. They'd had enough information from me.

When you're an understrapper they don't want to know, but if they take you into the fold it's another story. They ask about your partner, your family, your previous relationships, your friends. The security mob dig and don't tell, so you don't know what they have when you're being interviewed by Personnel. They don't stop prying; they don't stop digging. That's what they would have you believe.

Then, they suddenly stop asking questions, and that's quite effective.

Vetting is never finished – that's what they have you thinking. Never finished until everything is right in the head, and everything is never right in the head.

'Bring the shoebox,' Personnel tell you. They like a friendly rummage, in case one day you dirty your bib or go to the bad.

Their sudden silence is to tell you that they are ever vigilant, and to make it clear they think it's entirely credible that you will turn out to be 'a disappointment' – the technical term applied in such cases.

CHAPTER 2

I had a mental picture of Cecil, my old man – the elderly widower talking to himself alone in his house, narrating his life in short bursts as he made his way from the kitchen to his bedroom. I tried to keep that picture in mind as I drove to his house in Muswell Hill. There were changes I was making in his life as well as my own, and these were the result of some hard thinking. He had become frail – it seemed to me quite suddenly, though it couldn't have been so. He had taken a heavy fall from which he had recovered after a long spell with the help of Rita, an undeclared companion who was both kind and entirely unreliable. In the absence of Rita he and I had talked and together had made a practical decision.

I found him sitting at the kitchen table wearing his heavy coat and his hat. He was staring at a bowl of oranges in front of him. He scarcely glanced up at me when I entered. He was sitting upright, not slouching. He had his spine snug against the back of the hard chair. He was trying to be kind to his skeleton. To a stranger's eyes it would have appeared that his spirit had collapsed – had caved in. I knew this was not so. Behind his sad gaze he was still alert to any sudden possibility.

He had prepared himself for a long journey; an impossible journey forced upon him because, like everyone else, he had been unable to live a life without mistakes.

I told him he was looking well. He told me he was thirsty.

'Have one of those,' I said, pointing to the oranges.

He looked at me curiously.

'Or would you prefer a glass of water? I'll get you a glass of water.'

He reached out and picked up an orange and bit into it whole. The juice squirted from the corners of his mouth, dribbled down his chin, dropped on to the table.

'Have one yourself,' he said.

I didn't know whether I wanted to laugh or cry.

I patted him on the shoulder. 'We could go to the pub, if you want.'

'Have we time?' he asked.

'Yes. We've time.'

'You could do with a drink,' he said, and took another lunging bite.

We must have been charged by the fresh, sweet smell of orange because quite suddenly the next step was clear to us both.

He rose to his feet as quickly as he could manage. He didn't want assistance.

I can't speak of my feelings as I left him in the home. I can only say that he made it as easy as he could for me.

I had written the number for my mobile phone on an index card and given it to him. I had made sure that he understood he could call me any time, no matter where I was. I made it a joke – I lied and told him that I had given my number to Aunt Kate; that she had asked how she might contact me when she never knew where I was.

I caught a glimpse of my index card when he pulled out the contents of his pockets in his new room. I saw that the number, with 'Harry's mobile' written in my hand, had been supplemented. He had scrawled our surname under my given name.

Why had he done this, I wondered? There was no other Harry in his life. Then I realised he had added the surname because he thought some stranger might find him in a heap somewhere and go through his pockets. They would want a surname if they were to make a call.

'Come on,' he said, 'don't be hanging around here. You have work to do. Earn some money, for a change.'

He was forcing a smile.

I rang his sister-in-law, my promiscuous aunt Kate, in Dublin. I wanted to show him that the lines of communication were indeed open.

Ringing her, however, didn't please him. He started to pace up and down, allowing himself the shortest of tethers.

'Kate,' I said, 'it's Harry.'

'Harry. Have you found a woman? I have one for you.'

'Never mind that now.'

'But I do. I worry. It's not right. It's not healthy.'

'I'm on the case.'

'You're still with your friend's wife. Well, I suppose that's something.'

'We'll talk about me later. I'm here with Cecil.'

'Don't tell me he wants to talk to me, because I know you'd be lying, son. Put him on.'

I handed the phone to my father. Aunt Kate spoke loudly. I could hear what she was saying.

'Hello?' my father barked. There was no disputing that he was putting a question.

'Hello, Cecil. How are you, dear?'

'What's that supposed to mean?'

'You're keeping well?'

'Are you over here or over there?'

'I'm in Dublin. But I think I should come and visit.'

'Christ. You bloody Quakers.'

'Is it a nice place or is it a dump?'

'It's a dump.'

'Cecil . . .' I protested, but he waved me down.

'I'll have to visit.'

'It won't do either of us any good.'

'Never mind, dear. Never mind.'

'I don't need a visit, Kate. I don't need you poking your nose in.'

I could see he was touched by her concern.

'Did you hear me?' he asked. He didn't know which was his best ear for a mobile phone. He switched several times.

'I did, Cecil. What would you like me to bring? I've just had a win.'

'Harry,' he said to me, 'you talk to her. You tell her.'

What was I to tell her? That he had spent too much time on his own, and that he was now in decline? That he had been lost all these years without his wife? That Kate's

12

voice was too much like her sister's for it not to upset him? That he had forgotten others judged him by his behaviour, not by his unshared thoughts?

She knew all of this.

'No,' I said. I didn't take the phone from him, though he held it at arm's length in my direction. He wanted to hang up but didn't know how.

'Goodbye,' he called into the apparatus at the end of his extended arm. 'I'm going now.' He put it to his ear again and repeated that he was going. 'I've things to do.'

'I'll be over and you can show me everything is all right,' Kate said.

'I'm perfectly all right on my own. Don't bother me. Don't upset yourself.'

'A gansey and a bottle of Jameson. How does that sound?'

'Goodbye.'

'Goodbye, dear. I'll be talking to Harold. He said he'd meet me at the airport. He'll take me straight there.'

'Christ,' he said, glaring at me with firewater eyes. He handed me the phone. This time he pressed it into my hand. 'Tell her to stay where she is,' he barked, 'then turn her off.'

He marched over to the door, where he waited impatiently for me to finish.

'A big win, was it?' I asked Kate.

'It was, son.'

'I'll ring you again soon,' I told her.

'I've seen a lovely gansey,' she said. 'It's one with buttons down the shoulder.'

'Most of us cave in when we get old,' Cecil advised me when the telephone conversation was finally terminated. 'Your aunt Kate will explode. They'll be scraping bits of her off the walls. They'll be trying to piece her back together – as they do with crashed aeroplanes. I'll be able to tell them what they want to know. I'll be able to tell them why your aunt Kate burst. But they won't listen. And if they *do* listen, they won't believe me. When they have her bits in the plastic bag and they're none the wiser, I'll tell them she was burning the wrong fuel entirely. Too many fancy men. Too rich a mixture.'

Cecil saw me to the front door of the home, and I went to work with the old man's blessing.

There was the broader picture to take in. This was how the scenario was described to me. I've added a little colour to compensate for Bradley's dryness and for his overzealous application of the need-to-know principle. Bradley and his kind are afraid of being caught out. They want you to believe that their imaginations function only when speculating on margins and degrees. This gives them an air of wisdom. A wisdom that says I should get out more and see my friends, but then who will mind the shop? Who will be responsible?

Conservatism laced with false modesty and a prickly reserve. His sort are happier turning down an opportunity than taking a chance. So he would have you believe.

I was to learn otherwise.

It is difficult to counter that brand of wisdom. Difficult to counsel that it is worth taking a chance, because, for the most part, their caution is justified. Fundamentally, the Service is about containment.

Then, of course, when the Bradleys of this world do sanction action, everybody jumps. Everybody says a wise man has spoken and they set about their task.

Dealing with Bradley put you permanently on a slow, dangerous bend. He was not a field man, but he was a true professional. He knew the field and was a master of manipulation. When it suited him he could speak in one continuous sentence and all the words would be connected in such a way that they could be reeled back and repeated and still be the perfect mask through which, apparently, a divine perspective has been delivered.

That was my reading of Bradley's personality at that time.

'Harry,' he said as we drove in his car on that first day of work, 'I'm going to tell you a shocking story.'

His story took us to a golf course about twenty miles out of New York City. I start the picture with Captain Delaney of the New York City Police Department –

Captain Delaney saw the man in the soiled suit trying to throw up in the middle of the road ahead. Saw him sway madly and perform some dry retching but manage to stay rooted to the one spot. The captain maintained a steady speed. He was determined to be on the first tee by six a.m.

It was Saturday. He had had a clear run from his house in New Jersey through the Lincoln Tunnel, across midtown Manhattan, and over the Queensboro Bridge, and he wasn't about to stop for this sad klutz.

At that hour of the morning there was room to swing wide. He put on his indicator to give ample warning of his intention. If the drunk was going to lurch he would lurch towards the sidewalk. That was the reasonable assumption, but by no means a certainty.

The captain put on a spurt. If this guy was looking to get run over he wanted to wrong-foot him. There was no way he was stopping the car. Early morning was the only time that he and the others could get in a clean round of golf. He had the best part of twenty miles to drive and he was running a little late because his car wouldn't start. This was his wife's car he was driving. It was Japanese. He didn't like Japanese cars. He didn't like the way they handled. He didn't think it was right buying an import. It was bad for American auto-workers. He had tried to dissuade her from buying it but she had insisted it was exactly what she needed, and now he was forced to drive it to the golf club. This guy in the road had picked the wrong driver to make a drama with if that was his game.

Having given up on his own car the captain had been delayed a further ten minutes persuading his bleary-eyed wife that she could do without her car until late morning.

Usually he left the house before he was awake. His own car could get to the golf course by itself if there wasn't some idiot standing in the middle of the road. This kind of behaviour disgusted him. Sad people shouldn't be sad in the middle of the highway.

He was going to wind down the window and show his contempt by throwing the contents of his wife's ashtray in the guy's face, but then something in the way the man was shifting his weight on his hips made the captain change his mind and focus entirely on the main event. The drunk seemed to be making ready to jump right in his path.

At the last moment there was a little screech of tyres as the captain put his foot down on the gas and sped past on the inside.

The drunk made a wailing sound as the captain passed by in an instant. Only when the car was well clear did this guy cross his ankles and trip over himself and fall on his face. The captain saw him hit the ground in his rear-view mirror and hoped that it hurt.

The car climbed over a rise and he momentarily caught sight of the Manhattan skyline. This Japanese auto mirror was altogether too small, he decided. The city was partially shrouded in mist. The early morning sun blasted what was visible and Captain Delaney sighed with satisfaction. There was a screech of rubber from the car behind, but he made a point of focusing again on what was in front of him. All things considered, everything would be just right in his life if he could get his car fixed at the right price and his wife to stop smoking. If it were just pot once in a while, well, that he could share, but all that tobacco. All that filth in her lungs. It just wasn't right.

If he kept this speed he might make up the time. It was a magnificent morning to be out on the course. The engine noise bothered him. He had no sense of cruising. He thought he might put it to his wife that they should trade in both cars and spoil themselves. She could get something sporty. A car made in the USA.

Captain Mitchell, Detective Sergeant Adler and Desk Sergeant Shields were taking their golf bags out of the trunks of their cars in front of the clubhouse when Delaney pulled in. Everybody was smiling. Cops make this kind of synchronicity seem easy.

Theirs was a long-standing party and they were well matched. It was always a fiercely competitive game. At that hour there were no intrusions. For the duration of the round the two captains and the detective sergeant switched off their pagers and their cell phones and routed any emergency calls through the desk sergeant's cell phone. He could act as cut-out.

The mist that had cloaked Manhattan and spread thinly across the lower reaches of Long Island had now gone, but there were still white frost shadows in the lee of hedgerows, and there were still vivid green circular patches under trees where the frost had not fallen. The policemen's party set out on the first tee shortly after six. It was reassuring to know that if there were any criminals playing here they were quality criminals.

The grass was damp with dew. The balance between greenery, water and light seemed perfect. Somewhere in the distance a greenkeeper drove his lawn-mower over a gently undulating fairway. The sound carried a long distance on the clear air and made these men inhale deeply in expectation of the smell of cut grass. Membership fees were steep. You wanted a piece of everything that was going.

The policemen would have breakfast in the club-house after the game. God bless America's golf links. They teed off.

There was a rise leading to a plateau where the second hole was located. Mitchell was wide. His ball was in a bunker that rose in a lip to obscure half of the green from players on the fairway. Adler was on the edge of the green, together with Delaney. Delaney had played a particularly good shot and was nearest the pin. Shields was short with a stroke to play. They pulled their carts up the fairway to his ball and the others waited while he played his shot. He pitched the ball high. From that position they could see the top of the flag but not where the ball fell. It seemed to be as good a shot as Delaney's.

They climbed the rise leaving neat lines in the wet grass with their carts. When they came around the lip of the bunker and saw the green in its entirety for the first time they got a surprise. There was a man in a dark suit lying on his back, staring up at the sky. There was a starched white handkerchief in his top pocket. It looked like somebody else had stuffed it in there as an afterthought.

There were little pearls of dew on his eyelashes. His legs were straight and pulled apart. His arms were at right angles to his body and the palms of his hands faced up. His complexion was milky white. His lips were turning blue. There was a bullet hole in the centre of his forehead. There was very little blood on the forehead but there was a sizeable stain on the spongy grass from the exit wound in the back of his head.

The four men stood still for a moment taking in the scene. The sound of the mower carried on as before, but now there was a gentle breeze. The flag was fluttering. There was the smell of freshly cut grass.

'Fuck,' said Captain Delaney.

'Fuck,' confirmed Detective Sergeant Adler.

It was obvious to their professional eyes that the man

in the suit had been dead for some time. Whoever had done it was long gone. It looked like a professional hit. An execution.

It was Adler who took charge of the crime scene. He led the preliminary. Desk Sergeant Shields made the appropriate phone calls while the others drew ever closer to the dark shape, carefully examining the grass for clues.

When they got to the corpse Delaney went through the motions to ensure that life was extinct. Mitchell closed the corpse's eyes. There was nothing more they were prepared to do until the forensic team arrived, so they just looked at the body for a time.

'Nine-millimetre, I'd say,' said Adler. 'No sign of a struggle. No marks on the wrists. Nothing under the fingernails that I can see . . .'

Captain Delaney's eyes were wandering. It was odd seeing the three golf balls on the green and the one in the bunker in the same field of vision as the body. His mind was wandering, too. Had Shields's ball landed on the dead man's chest? Had it rolled towards the pin? Had it given him an advantage? Then he was thinking about the drunk in the middle of the road. Thinking how, with a little skill and determination, most obstacles could be got around. For some reason it was still a good day.

'So,' he said, 'are we going to finish this hole?'

'Are we what?' Adler asked.

'You heard him,' Mitchell said. 'My shot.'

'Hey,' said Adler, shrugging, 'you want to play through don't let me stop you.'

'You want to start the investigation?' Delaney asked.

'Hell, no.'

'Damn right.'

'It's just . . .' Adler jerked his thumb. 'It'll put me off my stroke.'

'This will be good for your game, Phil,' Delaney assured him. 'And he won't mind.'

'Nothing to be gained just sitting on our fannies waiting for the circus,' said Mitchell. 'We've done the preliminary, right? I'm the only one has to play over him and that's a clean clip out of that bunker. It's as good as in the hole.'

When Shields had done his business on his cell phone the cops finished the second hole. No mention was made of the possibility that Shields might have gained an advantage with his ball hopping off the dead man's chest. They did the sensible thing and played the balls as they lay. They took extra time measuring their respective shots and settling their feet for their putts. However determined the cop, it wasn't easy concentrating with a corpse stretched on the turf.

Captain Delaney won the hole. Presently, they could hear the wail of sirens above the sound of the mower.

CHAPTER 3

The man in the suit with the hole in his head was, as Jack Bradley described him, one of our gentleman spies. Bradley said that he was of the old school and that was the sort of thing that got a man shot in an awkward situation. That, and in this instance, the fact that the man in the suit was too tall. He hadn't been able to duck fast enough.

'Facts of life, Harry. Facts of life.'

I wasn't sure what that meant, but I gave a thoughtful nod.

'You'll like Johnny,' Bradley said, changing the subject to our immediate goal. 'He's a bit of a thug.'

We were stuck in traffic outside a shop that sold pairs of scales and bacon slicers. Rather than take Bradley's bait I attempted to rise to a more reflective plane. Could anybody make enough money out of selling scales and bacon slicers? The answer had to be that they could.

'A bit of a rogue,' Bradley added, 'but a good man to back you up in a tight fix. Very good on the practical skills, you'll see. And not too tall.'

The musing about scales and bacon slicers didn't go anywhere. 'What?' I said. 'He'll give me a demonstration of cooking a steak on a shovel over an open fire?'

'Certainly. He's got a good eye for detail, and he likes a bit of culture.'

'He knows the difference between a 300-year-old carpet and a roll of linoleum?'

'He does. And he watches the telly.'

'Better and better.'

'He's also a good thief. If Clements weren't so fussy I'd have you both in suits off the peg.'

'How do you mean – if Clements weren't so fussy?'

'You and Johnny have an appointment with the tailor. One of the very best, I might add.'

'I have my own suit, thank you.'

'Ah yes . . .' he said with a little downward inflection to indicate that he was thoroughly familiar with my suit and that it was a disappointment. The slight pursing of the lips said: I know the jacket pockets are like saddle bags, each one sagging with a big, dull grin. 'Why not have another? Something to fall back on. The very best of quality, and it won't cost you a penny – if we get it through before the annual audit.' He forced a brief laugh.

The annual audit. Now there was a work of fiction. Servicing, maintaining, oiling the wheels – it was an end in itself. Good money paid over to ensure that nothing much seemed to be happening. The politicians, the civil servants and, most especially, the Joint Intelligence Committee were happiest when it was reported that very little of consequence was happening. Sluggishness was not to be feared. On the contrary. It was a luxury that came with the kind of confidence placed in the firm generally. Clements and his heads of department were most comfortable when their political masters indulged themselves by wryly commenting that stagnation was the normal operational mode of their secret servants.

Clements nurtured their complacency in the knowledge that it was easily swept away by his merely raising
a faint, all-knowing smile at the right moment. His
critics would get a little thrill that shut them up. For
a remarkably long period thereafter they would exhibit
the patience of Job. Furthermore, this made it easier for
Clements to raise whatever suspicions he wanted with
the minimum of effort, and at minimal cost.

'So, when do I get details of the job?' I asked Bradley,
as he engaged first gear and we advanced twenty feet
before having to stop again.

'We'll get you and Johnny kitted out, then we'll
see.'

When I saw that we were turning off the motorway
into a service cafeteria my heart sank. I had many
unhappy memories of meetings in such places, getting instructions at unsociable hours from men and,
occasionally, women who felt no need to disguise their
loathing for the understrapper I once was.

'I'm not hungry,' I said curtly.

'I am.'

'We're meeting him here?'

'We are.'

'Doing a bit of socialising, are we?'

'Getting off to a good start.'

Bradley did a discreet scan of the customers as he
queued for his food. He got fish and chips with beans.
I got tea and toast. We sat down by a central aisle, away
from the plate-glass windows.

We ate in silence for some time, me trying to
learn what I could about Bradley's personality by the

way he tucked in. When he did speak he spoke casually.

'That's him over there. The dark-haired one with his leg going like a piston under the table.'

Johnny didn't know either of us by appearance. He had simply been given a time and meeting place and told that Bradley would find him. I took a look at him. He had both hands in the pockets of his car coat and he was staring at the people in the queue. I couldn't tell much over that distance but his leg cranked up a gear when he fixed on a young woman in a short skirt and black tights.

Bradley had already given me a scant biography. I asked him for more.

'Tell me about his time with the aid workers.'

'It didn't go well.'

'What? He turned up drunk? He's an alcoholic?'

'No. Very conscientious. Too conscientious.'

'Take them all out to dinner, did he?'

'No. As I've told you, he was part of the team teaching them how to deal with despot military men . . . Johnny was playing the baddy . . . rather too well.'

'You did tell me he was a thug. He doesn't look thick. He isn't thick, is he?'

'No. He just got carried away. Nothing too serious, apparently. Beat some of them around the place shouting at them that they didn't know what these men were capable of. The police were called. You can imagine.'

When we both glanced again in his direction, Johnny of the piston leg had vanished. Then, a voice came from behind:

'You gents looking for me?'

Bradley was unsettled by the ambush but covered it well. 'Thought I was going to have to whistle,' he said.

Fair play, Johnny, I thought, but his demonstration of stealth was wasted on us. He should have been more prudent, less trusting. For his own sake, he should have got to know us better before revealing his talents simply to impress.

'Harry,' Bradley said, 'meet Johnny. Johnny, this is Harry.'

We shook hands and he sat down beside me.

Bradley had a task for the too-conscientious and ever-vigilant Johnny, and it wasn't to make bagpipes out of a set of lungs and ribs – he would gladly have got to work immediately were that the job.

It was one of the standard humiliating exercises that the firm gave new recruits. It was ritual preparation.

'Johnny,' he said, putting on his special voice, 'do you see that porker of a lorry driver with the wide, sad eyes . . . ?' He stopped there and waited for a reply.

'What about him?'

Johnny was already scratching his chin discontentedly. He didn't turn straight away. When he did look it was only a quick glance at the target, then he was looking again at Bradley.

'I want you to talk to him.'

'Talk?'

'What's the matter? Just discovered you're wearing my dirty socks?'

Such observations were part of the tribal lexis. Even

Johnny knew this, so it didn't bother him unduly.

'Go and talk to him.'

'About what?'

'Interview him.'

I could see Johnny tighten up.

'Interrogate him?' Johnny said, putting an edge on it. 'You want to know where he's going and what he's carrying?'

'That . . . and more.'

Johnny cocked his head.

'Anything else you can find out.'

'How long have I got?'

'Well, now . . . he's shovelling his chips in at quite a rate, isn't he? My guess is he'll want to be back on the road by . . .' – he looked at his watch – 'twelve-thirty, wouldn't you say?'

'I'm sure you're right.'

'You might want to catch him outside.'

'I might.'

Bradley grinned. 'But we're leaving not later than twelve-twenty.'

Johnny sucked in his lower lip, bit down hard and nodded. He picked up my cup and saucer and rose to his feet. God had whispered in his ear and had told him to do Bradley's bidding.

He moved down the aisle towards the lorry driver. A coach party of short women with big hair and loud voices were blocking the way in a rush to get to the counter. He slipped through effortlessly.

Bradley let his head loll to one side.

'Some of the joes like this stuff,' he confided.

'And some don't,' I asserted. That didn't irk him.

He curled his lip. 'Rarely do a good job, though. Now Johnny, there, you can see he doesn't like doing it. He'll do better.'

Johnny didn't sit down directly at the lorry driver's table. Instead he returned to the service counter, where he refilled my cup from the stainless steel urn. He then moved along and picked up two rock buns from a pile.

'Are these today's?' he asked one of the staff behind the counter. He was told that they were fresh.

He walked away without paying. We watched as he sat down at the driver's table and attempted to ingratiate himself. A manager type who must have been all of nineteen came out from behind the counter to politely inform Johnny that he had neglected to pay. Bradley and I couldn't quite hear what was being said, but we observed Johnny making a token fuss and handing out some change. Once the boy manager had left, he got talking with the lorry driver on the back of the incident. Something along the lines of – I'm knackered. I've been driving non-stop for ten hours. Funny how under the politeness they think you're a thieving get.

Something like that.

Bradley concentrated on eating his fish and chips, and his beans. He had a system. He methodically pushed a piece of fish on to his fork first, followed by two chips, then piled a few beans on top. He was reverential about it. It was a show of patience.

I felt I shouldn't just sit there and say and do nothing, so I went to get myself another cup of tea. Which I paid for.

I took my time returning to our table. When I sat

down again with Bradley his eating became even slower and more reverential. I spent a long time stirring the sugar I hadn't put in the cup. It didn't bother old Jack. As if on cue, the moment Bradley finally put his knife and fork together on his empty plate, the lorry driver got up and went on his way. Johnny took some satisfaction in waiting a while before coming back to us. In the field, the agent is king.

'He's on his way to Dover. He's carrying sides of meat.'

'Meat?' Bradley came in quickly. 'What kind of meat? Beef? Pork? Mutton?'

'Beef.'

'Cows? Calves?'

'I don't know.'

'Is he English?'

'Irish.'

'Good for you. No trouble talking, then. Southerner or Northerner?'

'Southerner. He had a Dublin accent.'

'Lives here?'

'Hackney.'

'Nice chap, is he?'

Was there a right and a wrong answer to this? Johnny didn't know. In any case, he had no strong feeling either way, so he shrugged.

'Is he wearing deodorant?'

'Might be. I didn't get to sniff his pits.'

'Trainers or shoes?'

'Boots. Light boots. Brown.'

'How old is he?'

'Forty-six.'

'You're guessing.'

'It's a good guess.'

'Married?'

'Married. Two children.'

'Two boys?'

'"A boy and a child," he told me. The girl isn't sleeping. He needs to sleep. He's up very early for the long hauls. He's been giving her orange juice at bedtime and he's been putting rum in it. He hasn't told his wife.'

'Very good, Johnny,' Bradley commented with a forced air of tedium.

'It's twenty-five past twelve,' Johnny said, without looking at his watch. Instead, he looked back at the table he and the lorry driver had occupied. 'We should be going.'

Bradley grinned at me smugly. Johnny really didn't like having to do this kind of thing. He was indignant, but he had done well, just as Bradley had predicted.

'Change of plan,' said Bradley, taking a key off his key-ring and handing it to Johnny. 'I like it here. We're staying a little longer. You go out and find my car and sit in it until Harry and I have finished our little chat.'

Johnny took the key and stood where he was. Now he didn't feel so smart.

Bradley turned to me, then back again to Johnny. I could see Johnny wanted to ask which car was Bradley's, but thought better of it because he knew he would be humiliated further. Reluctantly, he moved away in the direction of what suddenly looked to be a very large assembly of parked cars.

Bradley settled in for a long talk about nothing in particular. I had no doubt that the key he had given my new partner didn't fit any lock in that car park.

CHAPTER 4

When I woke, the tip of my tongue prised my lips apart just enough to dampen the margins before withdrawing. I then worked my tongue over my teeth in one circular movement, stretched from the shoulder-blades, and performed a lockjaw yawn. I thought I was squinting because the morning light was too bright, but really it was because I had had my eyes shut too tightly all through the night and now they were reluctant to open wider than slits. My ears, however, had been awake a little longer.

I had been in New York in my sleep. I could still hear the honking of cabs. I was thinking through some of the details Bradley had given me. I could see hordes of cab drivers coming out of a boxing stadium. They'd been in a union meeting that hadn't gone well. They felt victimised. They felt they were being bullied by the Mayor's Office and the Police Department. There were raised voices, many of them chiding in broken English.

The police had been checking the ranks, searching the cars for illegal weapons. Cattle-prods, stun guns, iron bars, mace – they could get away with these, but unlicensed revolvers, pistols and zip guns were another matter. The drivers were angry at the searches. One of the men in the stadium, an Armenian, was thinking about the gun he had found on his back seat: five chambers containing shells, one empty. He had sniffed it. There had been the faint smell of cordite. He was assembling the face that went with the gun. The man who had paid the penalty fare to get him across the bridge from Jersey and as far as Grand Central Station.

Five shells, not six. It didn't necessarily mean a thing. Perhaps he only had five shells to load into his gun. But there was something about the face, something spiritual he thought, that suggested one bullet had been discharged and an evil purged. Now that he tried to conjure the man he realised that he could only make vague features stick. His was the face of an angel, and one angel's face was much like another's.

In any case, the taxi driver was sure he had done the right thing dropping the weapon in the river. He was as good a citizen as the next guy – wasn't he here in the boxing stadium with his brothers? He just didn't need anybody scrutinising his papers and asking him questions.

You can catch assassins in your sleep. A clue presents itself and, if you can stay asleep long enough with the excitement, you get to confront them close up.

It was early but I had to get up. There was the visit to the tailors to endure. Johnny and I had been told that off-the-peg wasn't an option. Bradley had made a fuss of giving me the name of a tailor in Savile Row and a judicious nod to indicate that I was to be responsible for Johnny getting it right.

As a general rule, a little vanity could save us all

a great deal of embarrassment, Bradley had observed dryly as he looked us both up and down in the car park of the motorway cafeteria. I could see that embarrassment interested Bradley. He was drawn to it like a shark to blood. It could be exploited. When a person was embarrassed they found it difficult to think on their feet, difficult to see beyond the moment, and that was a gift to an impatient inquisitor.

Johnny was already enraged by having to do the thing with the car keys. He had got redder still under Bradley's scrutiny of our clothes.

It didn't bother me. I had to admit that my own tarpaper suit was looking shabby. I would take up the offer of a new suit on the firm, I decided. I was thinking about dinner at the Ritz with my estranged wife, not about the job. Not about the Service.

Johnny and I met at the corner of Clifford Street.

'I hope this isn't going to take all day,' he said. He was nervous and didn't want it to show. He had never had a suit made for him and was assuming it would be a humiliating ordeal.

'I know what I like,' he went on, 'and that's what I'm getting.'

'You tell them.'

'I don't like to have the ends of my trousers riding up to my knees when I sit down. Know what I mean?'

He had put on his best pair of trousers for the encounter and it was obvious that they were to serve as an exact template.

'And I don't want a shiny arse. You know that kind of material – a month down the line and you have a bus driver's arse.'

'None of us wants that.'

'I could do with a new suit . . .'

'You talk to this tailor. He'll see you right.'

'I'll have to get a nice belt and a pair of Italian shoes . . .'

'No leather soles. You can't run in leather soles. You can't climb a drainpipe or cross a roof.'

'You think I'm stupid?'

'You don't see Chaps wearing belts. Too American.' I was referring to the monkeys the Service used.

'Fuck them.' Johnny hated Chaps as much as I did. He particularly loathed the confident public school twits – and they were all public school twits. Whatever their names, they were all called George.

'I'll want loops for a belt,' he insisted.

'Tell the tailor.'

'If I'm wearing a suit I'll want to look sharp. I don't want to look like some Whitehall lackey.'

'I'm sure this tailor will make a note of that.'

'Savile Row, eh . . . ?' Suddenly, he was overcome with the generosity of the Service.

'Only the best for you and me, Johnny.'

In many ways he was an innocent abroad.

I asked him if he had been interviewed by Clements.

No, but he had met him briefly in a corridor. Johnny was telling me that although he hadn't been properly introduced he had been smart enough to recognise the man.

'Did you see his toupee, Harry?'

'Everybody sees the toupee.'

'A master of disguise, our chief.'

'He takes his pullover off over his trousers.'

'That's reassuring.'

'While you're busy looking at his toupee he's looking inside your head.'

'Och, Jesus, Harry, what crap.'

'He knows you have a traffic cone on the mantelpiece of that kip you live in and that at two o'clock in the morning you're wandering the streets eating the fat end of your tie along with your kebab.'

'I don't wear ties.'

'Don't tell them that.'

'I think Bradley respects me for my talents.'

I couldn't decide whether or not he was joking. 'Does he?'

'Otherwise, I wouldn't get to work with you, right?'

'Can you run fast with your trousers around your ankles?'

'Christ. He's not a bender?'

'I wouldn't think you're his type, Johnny.'

There was nothing gay about Bradley, but suddenly Johnny wasn't sure. I was enjoying myself.

'What did he say about me? What's on my file?'

'He just asked if I liked working with animals.'

'I see. And you had a laugh?'

'It was a compliment. Which would you take hunting in the woods, Johnny, a professor of animal behaviour, or a dog?'

He basked in this for a moment. I knew he would like that.

'So. What's the job, Harry?'

'I don't know. We've to wear suits. Have you ever worn a suit?'

'I have a suit.'

'No you don't.'

'I fucking do. A four-buttoner.'

'Something you wear to the clubs, right? Well, you can forget it. That's why they have us going here.'

He was confused now. He was still thinking about being out in the woods on all fours.

'And a tie,' he added belatedly. 'Obviously *your* suit isn't up to scratch, either.'

'Hey – *I* have a real suit.'

'You haven't told me what he said about me.'

'We weren't talking about you. There were a few outstanding matters regarding my past.'

His face lit up immediately. 'You've caused trouble? You'll have to tell me.'

'"I've buried the hatchet," Bradley told me, "but I remember where I've buried it." Now, don't ask any more questions about it.'

'A suit, eh? Close protection, or beat up some barrow boy in the City? What do you think?'

'*And*, we have to do a medical.'

'A medical . . . ?'

A phone call had been made. We were expected. Mr Goodge, the tailor who attended to us, made it clear that it was so. There was something about him that suggested he had fallen from grace, but had done so with great dignity.

He was prepared, if not willing, to serve the likes of us. He did a lot of work for the civil service, he informed us, and it was almost always a pleasure.

I felt duty-bound to be a difficult customer. That way there would be more satisfaction in it for him when, finally, he had our measurements and we had our cloth. Johnny, I knew, would be challenge enough in the raw.

Mr Goodge politely gave us a cursory tour of the premises, showed us his entire range of fabrics, then politely informed us that one part of his telephone conversation with our benefactor was dedicated to limiting the choice of fabric available to us. We could have anything from the dark end of the spectrum, provided it was from the cheapest range.

Johnny ejaculated prematurely, spouting that he wanted a four-buttoner. Mr Goodge answered with an obliging, professional smile and a little dip of the head. He wasn't embarrassed at limiting us to the cheap range, because even at the cheap end the three of us knew that Johnny and I were going to come out ahead.

Johnny really got into the whole business and was soon marching up and down the shop, feeling the fabric, being familiar with Mr Goodge, and talking shite. I had to call him aside and have a word in his ear, because really, we were both put out. Both abased by our compulsory purchase. Furthermore, Johnny made it worse when he was being measured by misunderstanding Goodge's question.

'Does sir dress to the left, or to the right?' Goodge wanted to know.

Johnny thought he was asking under which oxter he wore a holster. I had to take him aside because the answer didn't tally.

'He wants to know which way you hang, you stupid bollix.'

'Oh.'

I suspect that Goodge had seen the error and had compensated for it in his notes. He decided he would flatter us, and, in the same instance, have fun at our expense.

'And does sir carry?'

Johnny looked at me. I returned a blank expression. He turned back to Goodge. 'Of course,' he replied self-consciously. 'Under the left arm.'

There was another professional smile from our tailor. I'd been measured first, but I hadn't had this treatment. Mr Goodge realised his mistake. He turned to me. 'Forgive me, sir, I should have asked you also.'

'He looks after me,' I replied. I tried to return the same professional smile.

Goodge gave another discreet dip of the head. He said that we could pick out two pairs of socks, and two white shirts each – from the discount pile of poplin.

'And what about ties?' I asked, much to Johnny's dismay.

'Ties. Yes, sir. Of course. I can offer you both ties.' He'd been told he should let us have a tie apiece if, in his opinion, we were men who obviously needed them. We needed them.

The choice was even more restricted than for the suit fabric. I could see Goodge was concerned that we would ask for old boys' ties to which we were not entitled. Or, that we would go beyond the budget.

'I want one with stripes going this way,' I told him.

'American, sir?'

'American stripes.' Apprentice John was impressed with this new information that the stripes on an

American's tie usually ran opposite to those on an Englishman's.

'One of them for me, too,' he said. 'Different colours.'

'Different colours,' Goodge echoed. 'We'll do our best, sir.' I imagine it was hard for him to smile professionally and nod, but he did so without hesitation.

Then, there was the medical.

It was an exceptionally muggy afternoon when I went to visit the spook doctor. The sun hadn't been able to break through and there was no wind, not even a light breeze. It had been like that for three days. It was a test of metropolitan life. There were people in the park banging drums as I made my way to the doctor's surgery.

'Show up on time, if you know what's good for you,' Bradley had said, taking a linen handkerchief from an inside pocket and mopping his brow.

He had been drinking, and he was doing his drunk matador act, which was his way of covering. He had me fixed with hooded eyes and was swaying slightly on his hips.

'What makes you think I'd be late?' I asked.

'Harry Fielding suits himself. That's what I've heard. Like a bloody criminal, eah, Harry? Look at the time. I really must be off. Traffic's murder.'

He still had me fixed with his hooded stare. Still swaying on his hips. 'I'm backing you. You know that.' He poked me in the stomach with a finger. I have always felt uncomfortable with such gestures. 'If you've had gonorrhoea or some other unspeakable disease, for

God's sake don't tell him because he will write it in his report. Scrupulous fellow is our Mr Robert. Don't tell him and he won't bother to check.'

In the tube on my way to see Dr Robert I was thinking about my father. Every morning now he had difficulty getting his feet into his socks. Shoes sat on the ground, their apertures ready to receive the feet. Socks did nothing of the kind. There could be no forcing the foot into the sock. He could curse. He might even give a terrible, short laugh. This oppressive heat, however, was another matter. It was an endurance test. He would soak in a bath until the water was cold rather than climb out to meet this fug.

Perhaps he had got up early, put on what he called his 'gutties' and gone to meet his cronies in the park where they talked and swapped their prescription drugs. It was so much better than collapsing back into a tepid bath because he 'hadn't the air'. Yes, he had forsaken the bath and, sockless in his grubby white runners, he had gone to sit with his mates.

I was thinking about the old man I suppose because, at last, I had what might be called a job. I was growing up. I was settling down. At last, I was seeing sense. I was putting things right. My serious transgressions were either being overlooked for the greater good, or were so well buried as to remain for ever undiscovered by my masters.

You see how dangerous that kind of muggy weather can be.

Dr Robert gave the impression that he had just come from someplace far more interesting than his own surgery and would be returning there as soon as he had attended to me.

'Dr Robert,' I said. 'As in the Beatles song.'

'Sorry?' He managed one of those aloof, slightly hurt looks.

'The successful Dr Robert . . . in the Beatles song. On *Rubber Soul* . . .'

The eyebrow which he had raised remained hitched while he gave the faintest of pained smiles.

If he was thinking I now felt like an idiot, he was wrong. I was determined I would not feel embarrassed, even with my oxters dripping and my trousers down around my ankles. I was healthy.

I had filled out a standard questionnaire and this he now read, taking a moment every so often to address a confirmatory remark to me.

'You've had treatment in hospital?'

'I had my appendix out when I was seventeen. And a few stitches in the head.'

He wanted dates and the hospitals at which these operations were performed.

On sexually transmitted diseases: 'Clean as a whistle?'

'Clean.'

On allergies: 'You've circled hay fever . . .'

'Mild,' I said. 'Three weeks in the year.'

On family medical history: 'Mother died, aged fifty-one. Cardiac arrest.'

'Yes.'

'Father still alive.'

'Yes.'

'Family doctor retired . . .'

'I can't remember the last time I went to a GP.'

'Not given to depression . . .'

'No.'

'Cheery disposition?'

'Something like that.'

I think he spotted that I had ticked the box for *Right-handed* with my left just for the hell of it, but he let it pass.

He started the practical by taking a blood sample. I knew that with the normal medical examination demanded by employers there had to be a specific reason to take a blood sample.

'Are you allowed to do that?' I asked.

'*I* am,' he replied, in a mildly indignant tone.

He caught me reading the remarks he had written on my questionnaire while he was drawing blood out of a vein in my arm.

'Good at reading upside down?'

'I try.'

'Very good.' He handed me a shallow plastic cup. 'I don't need much. Up the stairs to the next landing. Door on the left.'

I went upstairs, concentrated hard and pissed in his cup. When I brought it back he conducted an instant test and declared himself satisfied with the result. He then took my blood pressure and listened to my chest and my back with his stethoscope. When he was examining my ears he said: 'By the way, it's not on *Rubber Soul* . . .'

'What?'

'"Dr Robert". It's on *Revolver*.' He said that while he was looking through his ear instrument.

He tested my colour vision with cards. He checked my limbs for track marks, distracting me by asking if I was married.

'No.'

'Bachelor?'

'Christ, no.'

'Divorced?'

'Separated.'

'Girlfriend?'

'No.'

He smiled. 'All our singles say that.' He asked me to get up on the couch. 'Cheery but lonely chap?' he asked.

'No. Are these questions part of the medical?'

'Just trying to be friendly.'

He bent my right leg and tapped just below the knee with his rubber hammer, then told me to 'undo the trousers'.

'Do you want to know if I can shoot straight?' I asked.

'Certainly not. You shoot, do you?'

'No.'

He announced in a perfunctory manner that he was now going to examine my testicles. Somewhere in the procedure he mumbled, 'Sorry.'

'Right, you can get up and stand over there.' He pointed to a specific spot and went to wash his hands.

I knew he had put me there for the eye test. He had his back to me at the hand-basin so I took a few steps closer to the chart to read the smaller lines, just to smooth the way. I did it in a deft little move but when I turned I could see that he was watching me in the mirror above the sink. There was nothing disapproving in his expression. On the contrary. I felt another box had been favourably ticked. The Service likes an opportunist.

When he had dried his hands he went to the eye chart and flipped it over to present an entirely different configuration of letters. 'Right,' he said, 'the fourth line down . . .'

CHAPTER 5

The sun was still shining. There were old people scattered on the lawn, propped in plastic garden chairs. I saw what I have always feared in old age, something I cannot comprehend. I saw after a lifetime of experiences an isolation that belied those experiences; that would allow for so little of their extraordinary potential for exchange to be realised. It was evident in the positioning of the chairs. It seemed the only sustenance generated among the group was the small change of longevity. The routine of eating. The family visits. The waiting. The repeated feeble calling by the same few. Nurse. Nurse. And the others resolved not to call out.

A little shudder ran down my spine when I saw my father among them in his white plastic chair, looking and behaving like the rest. I was afraid that when I approached him he would be withdrawn. He would be lost. I would have to shake him until he felt he was having a religious experience. Until he was kicking. Until he was happy to be alive. I would draw him out, even if it killed him.

I drove slowly up to the house. I gave him a big wave, but he didn't see me. I beeped the horn. Waved again. They all looked in my direction. Several of them waved back. It still didn't register with him that it was me.

I pulled around by the rose-beds. Parked where I wasn't supposed to park. I wanted to be sure he saw me getting out of the car so that next time he would recognise it in an instant.

I got out and gave him another big wave, though he was only yards away.

'Hello, Cecil.'

Now he recognised me. He raised a hand. He was surprised to see me emerge from this vehicle.

'Harold . . .' he said, rising to his feet, 'you needn't have bothered coming. You're too busy.'

'I have the time,' I said. I had brought him a present of a new shirt and tie, two cans of Guinness and a tin of boiled sweets. I also brought him the newspapers. None of these was more interesting to him than the sight of the unfamiliar car.

'New car?' he asked, moving around me to inspect it. I was glad to see him engaged, even if it meant he did not recall his previous thorough inspection.

'Yes. I got a good deal.'

'I should think so.' He gazed in through a side window.

'Sit in,' I said. I flung open the driver's door.

'They don't like you parking here,' he said mischievously. His legs were weak. He climbed in unsteadily.

'Good condition.'

'Yes-yes.' He fiddled with the controls. 'Good performance?'

'Good performance. Good on petrol. Reliable.'

He reached down and released the bonnet catch. 'Tell you that, did they?'

I was heartened. He was sharper than my best

expectations had allowed for. 'You know how thorough I am, Cecil.'

'You never took enough interest in motors.' He climbed out of the car with some difficulty and blundered around to the front. I lifted the bonnet.

We both looked in. Neither of us spoke for a time. He poked about. He mumbled something about foreign engines. His voice seemed to desert him, but came back with a surge.

'You say you've bought this?'

'Yes. I've bought it. I haven't got it on trial.'

'A good price, was it?'

'Yes. A good price.' I gave him the figure. He baulked.

'They must be paying you well.' He was trying to show some pride.

'Any chance of a cup of tea around here?'

'Tea,' he exclaimed. 'I'm awash with tea. If you want tea, I'll get you tea.' He was angry at himself for being in this place. I had made all the arrangements, but he blamed himself.

He felt he should have another look at the car. He stepped back to examine the finish. 'How much?' he asked, but he asked as though it were the first time. I repeated the price. He was just as shocked the second time I told him how much it cost. We started walking towards the entrance. We were going inside for tea.

'They look after you well in here,' he said.

'I know they do.'

'I'm happy here.'

'I'm very glad.'

'They talk to you. They like to know where you've been.'

'You won't find better staff anywhere.'

'They look after you well in here,' he repeated.

'I know they do.'

He told me the food was good, then repeated himself almost immediately. Then he told me again that the nurses were very good.

When we entered the building he stopped and turned to me. 'Have you noticed there's a lot of magpies about?'

Yes. I had noticed.

He told me that the grounds were extensive, and that there was a great variety of trees and shrubs which attracted a great abundance of birds. He watched the birds. Had I noticed how many magpies there were? Aggressive buggers, but many of the smaller birds were persistent in spite of the magpies.

His short-term memory was failing him, yet his repetition didn't have the lack of concentration that I associated with forgetfulness.

He stood in the hallway with his feet apart and looked to the left, then to the right. For the moment he could think of no particular reason to move in either direction. The sight put a lump in my throat.

'This way,' I said tentatively.

'Yes. Of course.' Still unsure, he led the way without further hesitation.

A nurse greeted him by name and that reassured him. He wanted to leave what I had brought him in his room. The room was oppressively hot, but he didn't seem to notice.

'I'm going to open the window,' I said.

'You do that,' he replied, while he coped with the question of whether or not the things I had brought him should all be stored together. He decided that the new shirt, the tie and the sweets could be separated from the Guinness and the newspapers. The shirt, tie and sweets were put in the wardrobe.

I opened the window. The sound of an ambulance siren passing in the distance came in on the breeze. My father paused to take in the sound.

'Poor bastard,' he said, putting the Guinness in the hand-basin. 'There's another job going vacant.' He spoke succinctly. He was telling me that he was still connected to the world. He set his mouth in a thin, straight line and scanned the headlines conspicuously before folding the newspapers and placing them on his bed. The presence of an outside world – a newspaper – seemed to confirm that he should be guarding against a shrinking existence.

'I seem to be in some kind of women's place here,' he said.

It was a valid observation. Seventy per cent or more of the residents were female.

'Have you any idea how difficult it was for me to arrange that?' I replied, forcing a joke.

He gave an amused snort, but it wasn't difficult at all to grasp the statistics. We both knew that the majority of women outlived the majority of men. There comes a point in old age when many men just give up and turn their faces to the wall.

'Half of them are batty,' he said with a moderate sigh. 'Just like your aunt. Christ, now that I've mentioned her she's sure to show up.'

That was his way of asking if I had been in touch with his sister-in-law Kate. Though he railed at her he cared enormously what she thought of him. And I think he felt ashamed that she would be coming to visit him in a nursing home – in this women's place. She would look at him and she would see through his shaky preening, his exercising and his loud bluster. She would come out with some nonsense about him thinking that his lying invigorated him, made him stronger – the more noble the cause the greater his strength – but no amount of lying would disguise the fact that, really, he was desperate for her attention, but resigned to his predicament. A very old man in a typhoon suit.

She would, he believed, turn up and announce that any prospect of them having a sexual relationship had long passed and it was his fault for not having made a move and that now he would have to be content with jam sandwiches and mashed bananas with the cream from the top of the milk bottle for gratification until it was time, as she would put it, to wear a marble hat.

She would, he believed, taunt him about his earlier life when he surrounded himself with scruff – opportunists, good-time Charlies – who looked up to him. She might even suggest that he had married the wrong sister and had compounded his mistake by not marrying the other after his wife died.

Cecil's weakness for the company of scruff was exceeded only by his desire to court Kate, an enduring desire upon which he had never acted. I had not asked him about this. I could only conclude it was out of loyalty to my long dead mother.

'Your aunt Kate would be very much at home here,' he assured me. 'Rule the roost, she would, without them ever knowing it.'

He had been in love with his promiscuous Irish Quaker sister-in-law for many years. There was a silence that ran under our conversation and in that silence he seemed to be watching for her, dreaming a dream that could not be cut short or interrupted. I imagined it made his day shrink. Progressively, there seemed to be more at stake.

'You've seen her recently?' he asked. 'You've been in Ireland?'

'No, but I talked to her again on the phone.'

'*You* rang *her*?'

'Well, yes . . .'

'To talk about me?'

'Among other things . . .'

'Don't tell me – she's remarkably well?'

'She's getting on, too, Cecil. She's not as well as she used to be.'

'They'll have to shoot her. You rang – and she was in? She wasn't out gallivanting? She must be slowing up.'

'She wanted to know all about you.'

'It's disgusting at her age.'

'Yes, I know. You've told me.'

'What did you tell her?'

'Nothing much,' I lied. 'That you were convalescing.'

'Good.'

He was afraid that she would say she used to think of him as a man with a deeply inquisitive mind and no interest in himself, but that time had proved him to be selfish and dull-witted.

'She's definitely coming to visit you.'

'Christ.'

I have this friend at the airport. He used to keep me supplied with on-board dinners, but that dried up. There was some kind of audit. Some rationalisation. He still can't get me cheap fares or upgrade my ticket, but he can get me long strips of the hard-wearing narrow-gauge carpet that is manufactured for aeroplane aisles.

Bradley and I took off from Heathrow for New York, and banking over the city, I looked down into the suburban gardens. The old man had been spending more time in his garden shed, wrapped in his coat and wearing two pullovers. I was thinking I could get these strips of carpet, cut them to size and insulate the shed. I was fooling myself that there was a chance he would regain his strength. That he would get home again.

I would have to call my friend when I got back.

Returning to London from self-imposed exile had given me new hope. But it had also forced me to take a cold, long look at reality. There was a price to pay and I thought about that on the plane to New York. The rift between my wife and me had brought a boundless exhaustion, and this in turn had bred a laziness that might be classified as grief. It was also a defence against all the good that might have passed between us had we remained together.

I had been going to places we used to frequent; shared favourite places. I was surprised that these visits had no real effect. They took me no closer to her and I had to empty my mind to record a few irrelevant details of my surroundings – a small ink stain on the trousers of a new head waiter; a piece of glass missing from the stained-glass window in a gin palace; wind making the leaves shake above a path in the park.

She did not exist in these places. The reality did not come back. Nothing got any clearer. I am a good observer, yet I could sense nothing but a glorious, unbeatable indifference.

I had taken a notion to visit the street where I had lived when I was an understrapper for the firm. I thought I might stand outside the block and look into the ground-floor flat and learn something about myself. I had lived there alone. It had been my watch-tower. From this place I had set out to take questionable actions in the name of a greater good, and that hadn't bothered me.

Now that I was older, wiser and had a pensionable job, I was more hesitant and had more scruples. I needed to get back some mettle.

I parked the car some way down the street. There is a grass patch in front of the block. As I approached on foot, from a distance I observed a woman in her sixties exercising on the grass; in itself, not altogether unusual. After all, they did it in droves in China. But this wasn't t'ai chi. This wasn't eurhythmics for pensioners. It was still muggy outside. The buses were leaning up against each other, but she was dressed in her coat and hat and heavy stockings and fleece-lined shoes.

There was something alarming in her intent. She ran with more agility than you might expect, then she stopped and stretched, putting her hands on her hips and arching her back. She made other jerky movements which suggested that she was doing this without any kind of instruction. She was probably doing more damage than good.

She ran back and forth over the same patch of grass, stopping at each turn–about to do her stretching exercises. They were getting progressively more erratic.

Somebody should do something, I thought. Somebody should tell her to stop. She wasn't benefiting from the expenditure of energy. The jerky stretching was causing pain.

I shouted. The words came out of my mouth without warning.

'On you go. Very good . . .'

She glanced at me, and in her glance I saw a weary panic. There was also complete acceptance of my jolly goading. I recognised her with that glance. It was Mrs Lamb, a former neighbour. My eagle-eyed watcher.

'Well hello, Mrs Lamb . . .'

'Harry . . .' She was happy to see me. Happy, at least, to see a familiar face.

'What's this you're at?' I asked.

'I'm keeping fit.'

'You should take your coat off to do that.'

She was out of breath. 'Finished now for today,' she said. 'Come and sit down. You're not in a hurry, are you?'

She led me to what she called 'the dead man's bench'. It had a memorial plaque set in the backrest. Captain Somebody-or-other.

'We'll go inside in a minute,' she said. 'Just let me catch my breath.'

'Of course. Take your time.'

'Something wrong, Harry?'

She seemed very much older than I remembered, but still full of fight; still alert.

'No. Nothing wrong.'

She liked the company of men, and she liked to show this with a confidential directness.

'It hasn't been the same since you moved out. Never got your deposit back, did you?'

'No.'

'Bastards want me out.'

'And how long have you got?'

'As long as I like, love. I'm not moving.'

I had to smile.

'Are you in trouble?' She took a quick glance over my shoulder.

'No.'

'Right, then.' She unbuttoned her coat, but kept it on. 'We can stay out here a little longer. I need the air.'

'We're not moving until you're ready.'

'You're looking well. You didn't get married, did you?'

'No.'

'I'm looking for a day out.'

'If it happens you'll get an invitation. I promise.'

'I kept your post for you. Rubbish, what there is of it. I have it inside.'

'Thanks for doing that.'

'She was right. The post was only rubbish. She

said there had been no callers looking for a Harry Fielding. If there had, she would have known about it, she insisted.

I asked if she had been paying her rent when it was due. She didn't see my question as prying. She had told me before that there were times in the past when she had delayed paying. When she was rowing with the landlord.

No. She was up to date.

'But you're on the tenants' committee. They can't throw you out.'

'Used to be, love. I used to be chair.'

'But you had a row?'

'They don't like me, Harry. You know that.' She gave a little evil grin. 'They think I tell lies.'

'Only when you have to, right?'

'Right. But you try telling them that.'

'So, you're rowing with the landlord *and* the tenants' committee?'

'You know who's running it now? The madman in Number Twenty-one. Have you noticed how madmen have great tufts of hair?'

'I have.'

'I've had enough air. Come in.'

She got up and led the way into her flat. 'I haven't much I can give you. I'm having a milk stout myself. It's part of my new health routine. They used to give it to you when you were lying in. After you've had the baby. Full of iron.' She was babbling away but that was something of a cover. I caught her glancing left and right to see if anybody was watching. She wasn't convinced by my protestations of being free of trouble. 'I hear some of them eat the placenta these days. Wouldn't catch me at that.'

She had trouble opening the door with her key. She didn't want me to see that her hands had become arthritic. I pretended not to see her struggle.

'What's a milk stout?'

'What it says. Half milk. Half stout.'

'No thanks.'

'It's all right. I have a drop of whiskey for you.' She succeeded in turning the key. She pushed the door in. It gave a loud creak as it swung on its hinges.

She spoke over her shoulder. 'That's another thing – the madman wants me to oil the hinges on my door. He says it distracts him from his work. I'm not going to tell him I want them squeaking for security. I'm not going to tell the madman who lives upstairs that, am I, Harry.'

'No. You're not.'

Her flat was more run-down than before, but it was still arranged for comfort.

She took off her coat and draped it over a kitchen chair. She had no difficulty opening the bottle of Guinness. She made her milk stout and poured a generous measure of whiskey.

'Had a delivery the other day . . .'

'Oh yes?'

'Four hundred bread rolls.'

'What?'

'Four hundred bread rolls. The delivery man wouldn't take no for an answer. 'They're not for me, darling,' I told him. 'I don't eat much bread. I never eat rolls.' But he shows me this docket he has with my address on it.

So, he put these four plastic bags down on the floor – right there where you're standing. I left them there for two days. Then the gentleman who's living in your flat knocked on my door and asked if I'd taken a delivery. They were his, you see. I think he runs some kind of a take-away business. Hot dogs, and that.' She was over by the window now, glass in hand, just making sure I hadn't been followed. 'There's a lot of money to be made in that game.'

We sat and talked for a time. She soon moved from the milk stout on to the whiskey.

'Don't think I'm getting drunk with you, because I'm not,' she announced. 'That will have to be another time, when you've got yourself sorted.'

I wasn't sure what exactly she meant by getting myself sorted, but it made her feel good believing she still had work to do looking out for my back.

I should have told Bradley that she would be a good person to have with us in New York, never mind the firm's dogs.

CHAPTER 6

It was to be a short visit to New York. There was an official but secretive part. Then, there was another encounter altogether. We started with the latter first. From JFK, we took the A train to our clandestine rendezvous. We transferred to the local L line and rode all the way to First Avenue, where we surfaced, crossed the street and descended to the other platform as instructed. And there we waited. There was a long gap between trains. It was mid morning. For New York, it didn't seem like a lot of people in the station. Bradley didn't say a word, so I kept quiet.

We observed a man advancing towards us. He was carrying a large trout curled in the bottom of a blue plastic carrier bag through which the light of one of the scarce oncoming trains shone as he drew closer. He had a clapped-out professional air about him, was unshaven and wore a greasy hat. A disbarred doctor or grubby lawyer, you might think. The kind who would tell you he catches fish in a plastic carrier bag.

He was looking at us and wasn't shy about it, but I could see he was short-sighted. There was something in the way he shambled along that told me those glasses he should be wearing were lost or broken.

'Ah-ha,' said Bradley.

'You're not serious.' He wasn't at all how I had

imagined him. I had him much sharper-looking, more hawk-like.

'Yes. This is our man.'

This was the cop we had been waiting for. Our Detective Sergeant Adler, NYPD.

Adler nodded, or rather, he pulled in his chin momentarily and gave us a guttural grunt. His breath smelled of garlic, the pungent metallic thwack you get from cheap, cured sausages.

'You know me?' he asked precisely.

'I feel we do,' replied Bradley, with a little display of facial tics.

'Well then, we can get straight to the point.'

'We can, of course, Sergeant,' Bradley said, with a warm wash of satisfaction that was carbonated with excitement. 'We can get right down to business.'

It was uncanny. With each exchange he was behaving and sounding more like Clements. He was hugely bright and had many skills. He was pretending to be clumsy in the field. I think he was playing it as he thought Clements might play it – too eager.

Scruff-bag Sergeant Adler, on the other hand, had nothing to prove and the sound of his voice had the assurance of a tugboat engine. He did, however, have something to tell us.

Bradley put out his hand and began to introduce us with spurious names, but Sergeant Adler interrupted.

'I don't want to know your names,' he said, with the same downbeat precision. 'And I don't have much to say,' he held up the carrier bag with the fish, 'which suits me fine.'

He did shake our hands. One firm downward stroke each.

I was wrong about him being a miracle fisherman, I decided. If anybody could catch fish in a plastic bag it was this obdurate, patient man who today was in a hurry to get cooking. He ushered us on to the Brooklyn-bound train just before the doors shut.

He waited for us to sit down first. There were spaces opposite, but he chose to sit beside us.

'You see this train,' he said, sprawling. 'I don't know anybody who rides this train.'

'Really?' replied Bradley, showing far too much bogus interest.

Adler didn't give a damn. He was just breaking the ice with a sledgehammer.

It was convenient, of course, that he didn't know people who travelled on this line. It made him feel slightly more comfortable.

'We're under the East River right now,' he said, with a quick jerk of his eyes upwards.

Bradley made a point of looking up with an air of wonder.

Adler wasn't sure just how impressive this feat of engineering was, but I did detect a trace of pride. It was as if he were telling us his wife had come home to him yesterday having had a Brazilian wax job done.

We were embassy officials, as far as he knew. That was how he had made contact, through the embassy. He was smart enough to know that we weren't from the visa section.

'I'm taking a risk here, right?' he said, lowering his

voice so that it was barely audible above the racket of the train.

Bradley nodded gravely, making sure to maintain eye contact, and Adler told his story. The cops knew that the man in the suit was a British civil servant based in the embassy in Washington, and were convinced that he was a man with a secret mission.

Bradley shrugged.

Adler got to the point. 'You want to know who killed this man and we're telling you we don't know. Well, we do know who did it. We made an arrest. But we had to let him go. The Feds put him on a plane to Amsterdam. God knows where he went from there.'

He passed an envelope to Bradley. 'Here's his picture.'

Bradley didn't take the envelope. I had to reach out for it. Bradley just held him with his gaze. Adler understood this for the question it was – why divulge this information?

But there was no answer. Adler just looked down into his blue plastic bag and let the rocking motion of the train set it swinging between his legs.

He didn't strike me as a man with a grudge. Maybe he was just an honest cop who wanted to see justice done.

After a long pause, Bradley thanked him.

'Yeah, right,' Sergeant Adler replied despondently. 'You do the right thing.' He rose to his feet and made his way through into the next carriage. I looked to Bradley to see if he wanted me to follow him, but he shook his head.

He took the envelope from me and slipped it into his coat pocket.

I got the impression that Bradley already knew the face in the photograph, and that the good sergeant had merely confirmed what he already knew. It wasn't my place to ask, but I asked anyway. I was getting hot in my new suit.

'We know who it is, don't we?' I was using the royal 'we'.

'We do.' Naturally, this royal 'we' excluded me. I was his new charge. His apprentice. He was going to teach me well. That was why he was smiling to himself.

According to a brief report in the newspaper, the NYPD line of enquiry centred on an unlikely but actual alliance between New York-based Hindus and radical Jews whose anti-Muslim activities were being monitored by the FBI. The theory was that the dead man in the suit was known to be involved in the arms trade and had been negotiating the sale of sophisticated weapons to the Arabs.

Some of these Hindus had marched alongside Jews in the annual 'Salute to Israel' parade down Fifth Avenue, and some of these Jews had joined in protests outside the UN building against the treatment of Hindus in Afghanistan by Muslim fundamentalists.

Neither group was responsible for the corpse in the suit on the putting green. The firm knew that. The NYPD knew it, and so, too, did the FBI.

While Sergeant Adler was frying his fish Bradley and I went about the other business. In spite of the body being found on a golf course on Long Island, somebody at the embassy had arranged for it to be brought to Manhattan, to the coroner's morgue on First Avenue, so that was where we went.

We gathered at a wall of freezer cabinets. There was the Coroner's Office official, two plodders from the FBI, Captain Delaney, a detective from the local precinct, a mortuary attendant, Bradley and me. As far as the others were concerned, we two were from the embassy. Bradley was expert at playing a first secretary.

The mortuary man pulled out the drawer. There he was. Our man in the suit. Our man with a small calibre bullet hole in his forehead. It was just as I had imagined it would be, except they had taken the suit off, and they had retrieved the bullet via an incision in the back of the neck. The trajectory of a small calibre bullet can be repeatedly altered by striking bone in a body.

He looked peaceful, which was ridiculous when you consider what had happened.

I should have been concentrating on the job. I should have been giving my undivided attention to our man on the slab. Instead, I was thinking about my friend Alfie. Husband of my friend Ruth. One day they would find Alfie's body, but I would continue with my pretence that I knew nothing of his fate until the dreadful news had come from the police.

I was carrying this secret – I knew my crooked copper friend Alfie had been murdered, and I hadn't been able to tell Ruth. There was a Missing Person file open on him. Aside from the thugs who did it, so far as I was aware only I knew Alfie had been killed. I had seen the danger but had been powerless to prevent the killing. I couldn't tell Ruth because of my job as an understrapper. I couldn't tell anybody. For selfish motives I had concealed that truth, and now I stared at the face of this stranger and could only think of Alfie.

Don't start talking, Alfie. It's my experience that when dead men decide to talk it's hard to get them to stop.

I know what you're saying, Harry.

Shut it.

I'm a dead man, Harry, and since I departed we haven't had a good talk. You haven't been prepared to listen, have you, old pal? You haven't given me even a little time driving around in your car.

Captain Delaney asked if I could make a formal identification. As per my instructions, I lied and said that I could. Before leaving London I'd been shown a photograph of our man without the hole in his head. They'd dug it out of the files in Personnel.

I can look up my wife's dress, Alfie said, but I can't get to talk with you.

I made a brief statement formally identifying our man and everybody was satisfied.

'It's just as we found him,' Delaney said. 'Flat on his back, but peaceful looking, like he'd been whacked with a feather.'

I'm in a filthy culvert, what's left of me, and you're not talking to Ruth either, but I know you would never forgive me if I didn't go to you with my troubles, Harry.

'Come this way, please, sir,' said the mortuary official with a broad sweep of his hand. He led the party into his

66

office and from an ante-room brought us the suit and the other clothing. The Long Island cops had bagged the contents of his pockets and had sent the stuff along with the body.

It's just like your suit, Alfie said. I expect it comes with the job. I'm your dead friend. Talk.

The suit was given to me. What was I to do with it? Give it to his family? Return it to the firm. It might fit one of the Georges, and who would be any the wiser if it was passed to the new recruit by the firm's tailor?

'Thank you. I'll see this is taken care of.' What was I saying?

Alfie let out a deafening whistle for me from his culvert while the mortuary official went through the arrangements for the transportation of the body.

Bradley had a meeting with two CIA spooks. I was excluded. He was afraid we would miss our flight so we had dinner at the airport. That was where he told me something of the larger picture. The shooting of our man in the suit marked the end of a chase, for a time at least. Target A was described to me as a former Balkans warlord and despot claiming to have a Russian-made nuclear suitcase-bomb for sale. Several attempts to trap him had failed, and this was the latest attempt. The operation had begun in London and had ended on the golf course in Long Island. Our man in the suit had been hot on the trail of compromising information and had got himself a bullet in the head for his trouble. Whoever had shot him wasn't arrested, as Sergeant Adler had believed, but had been allowed to run and then followed. The photograph he had produced was an old one from police files. Adler had not been part of the police investigation. Long Island wasn't his beat. Everything he had was second-hand.

To have arrested the suspect would have alerted Target A. There would be another chance, Bradley assured me. Something was already in train. He wouldn't say what, just that Johnny and I had a role in it.

I knew from a brief encounter with Bradley in my days as an understrapper that he practised lying. That is to say, he practised to keep on form. He lied when he didn't need to lie, which is not the same as being a compulsive liar. It is something close to the opposite. So far as I could judge, his lying was rarely about hard facts.

'You had your chance and you didn't take it,' he might say, and you wondered, did I – did I have my chance? And then, you began to doubt.

Everything he told me had to be weighed, thought through, reconsidered, and he knew it. That was part of his mentoring now.

For all the games that were played, the firm was peopled by civil servants and as such relied absolutely on a sense of security and privilege. That meant being accountable absolutely as they saw fit. It suited the machinery of government. The slower the firm changed, the more efficient it was deemed to be. This, at any rate, was the notion encouraged by Clements and others and was, of course, an effective screen for the small but significant changes that were made on a regular basis.

We are the best at what we do is inevitably the most potent argument for self-regulation. The king always has the best rope. We can only be replaced with something inferior.

So, who was going to be held accountable for the action against Target A failing? Who was going to question our First Class transatlantic tickets? Only Clements and the firm's own bean counters.

As the jet took off and I was pressed into my seat I thought again about the strips of carpet, but the reality of the old man being permanently in the home asserted itself.

Then, I thought about my ex-wife, whom I was going to win back.

CHAPTER 7

I visited my father on his desert island. He wondered how I had got there.

'What are you doing here?' he asked. His demeanour told me that each time I visited he would be surprised to see me.

'I've been looking forward to seeing you,' I replied. He didn't ask if I had come to rescue him or to smother him with a pillow. Instead, he smiled conspiratorially. There was a moment of silence between us. He looked about, a little confused, a little disappointed, as though the cocktail hour had been cancelled. I put my hand on his shoulder.

'This way,' he said, and I followed. He wanted to impress me with his walking; to show me that some of the power he had lost in his legs had returned. I kept my hands out of my pockets in case he stumbled.

'Where's your coat?' I asked before we left his room. 'It's cold. You'll need your coat.'

He told me he didn't have a coat with him. Would I bring him his coat from the house?

'It's here in the wardrobe,' I told him. I opened the wardrobe door.

'That's not my coat,' he replied emphatically.

'I got you that new coat,' I told him. 'It's brown. Like your old coat.'

There were other clothes in the wardrobe that weren't his, he told me. They belonged to the previous occupant.

'I bought you that new brown coat,' I said. 'You told me you liked it.'

'It might be brown,' he said, 'but it isn't mine. I want *my* coat.' He didn't want somebody else's coat, he insisted. He wanted *his* brown coat. Would I bring it next time I visited? It was hanging up in the hall. If it wasn't hanging in the hall it was draped over the banisters, but he was sure that it was in the hall.

I told him that I would bring him his coat. I persuaded him to wear the new coat. He sorted through the clothes that hung in the wardrobe clearly convinced that they did not belong to him.

He put on his new coat. He seemed surprised that it fitted him.

He was in a foul mood. 'If anybody is looking for me I'm out,' he announced gruffly to the old man who was sitting by himself in the television room beside the main entrance. Mistaking this for an invitation, the old fellow told Cecil that he wanted to go out but couldn't. There was something wrong with his Zimmer frame.

'What do you mean, it isn't working?' Cecil demanded, turning on him. 'There's nothing wrong with the frame. How could there be something wrong with the frame, you bloody old fool?'

He immediately regretted his sudden cruelty and got choked up.

I led him out of the room.

'I shouldn't have said that,' he confided as we shuffled into the open, 'but he should count himself lucky.'

He didn't mean what he said about being lucky. We both knew that he wasn't in a position to judge, one way or the other.

Out in the grounds he pointed to a gentle incline on one of the garden paths. He told me he tramped up and down that for exercise. To make him well again.

It was a scene that would be repeated often.

In spite of his own troubles he was worried about me. He lost his way, or rather, forgot where he was taking me.

'I'm looking forward to this cup of tea,' I said.

'Tea,' he exclaimed, 'plenty of that here.' He had found his way again.

He was making a determined effort to stay outdoors as much as he could. It was part of his survival strategy. It had been raining all morning and all afternoon. I had been wondering what he would do when the first rainy day came.

He told me he had spent the afternoon watching crocodiles eat wildebeest.

On the telly.

Then he asked about my wife and suddenly it was time for me to leave.

He chose not to take the lift or the electric chair but to climb the staircase ahead of me. He gripped the banister firmly and forced the motor function of his leg muscles.

'Are you all right getting up these stairs?' he asked, without looking back.

I thought at first that he had momentarily forgotten that it was his son who was following, not a fellow resident, but when he turned to see why I had made no reply, I knew this was not so.

That he should confuse his condition with my good health was a keen surprise. That he should care in spite of his fears for his own failing health was touching.

'I'm fine, Cecil.'

'There's a spare bed here in my room if you find yourself stuck,' he said, slowing as he turned on to the next flight of stairs. 'You could stay a night or two. I don't know what the arrangements would be about food.'

He passed this invitation off in a casual tone in case I might think he would be anything but easy company.

I thanked him, told him it was good to know that there was a bolt-hole. This pleased him.

Apprentice John wrestled with his suit. He ran his fingers around the inside of the waistband in an effort to tuck in a shirt which was two sizes too big for him.

'It's like being in The Beatles, man, with these poxy suits,' he complained.

In my experience it's always an advantage to be well dressed when you're in a bad mood.

He made sure I saw the flick-knife in the neat leather scabbard that was clipped to his belt at the small of his back. He was testing my reaction, not looking for permission. We were hanging around the car pool in our suits, waiting for Bradley.

'What's that for?' I felt obliged to ask. Officially, if there was need for a flick-knife it would be registered and formally issued. Curiously, the firm was as particular about knives as it was about guns. There was an officious edge to my question. There was also the ring of hypocrisy, for I had been in the practice of keeping

73

my own weapon – a small automatic. These were new circumstances, I told myself. Nothing wrong with being smarter than the next man.

'You never know,' he said flatly.

'You never know what?'

'You never know, do you?'

Furthermore, I was mindful of Apprentice John having flown off the handle during his little improvisation for the aid workers. I would have to ask him about that.

'You don't need a knife,' I said.

'How do you know?'

'Is there an echo in here?'

'How do I know what I need?'

'Stash it. We draw down what we need.'

'It's stashed,' he said, pulling on the scabbard.

'I'm telling you not to carry it. Put it somewhere safe.'

'It's safe with me, Harry. You can't tell what might happen . . .'

'Keep it under your pillow at night, do you?' I asked, trying to make him feel foolish.

'You wouldn't know.'

Bradley finally emerged behind the wheel of a Ford saloon. He drove us to a street in Pimlico. He gave a twitch of the head.

'That one there . . .' he said.

We passed the house twice before he pulled in to the curb some way up the street. Then he gave us a brief lecture on being discreet which began with 'Now, I know I need hardly tell either of you this . . .'

'You want us to, ehhh . . .' – Apprentice John spoke

out of turn but finished his sentence awkwardly – 'do a job, like.' He wasn't sure what the firm jargon was, so he wound his hand in the air and darted a glance at the house. His earnestness was quite touching.

'Harry,' Bradley said turning to me, 'what do I want?'

'You want to know who comes and goes.'

'And?'

'You want photographs.'

'And?'

'You want to know what happens in the house.'

'You want us to break in?' Apprentice John said, again speaking out of turn, but growing in confidence.

Bradley looked at Johnny with a pained expression, and then again at me.

'Yes, right, of course, sorry . . .' said Johnny, suddenly feeling foolish. For all his street experience he was really quite naïve when it came to judging what exactly was expected of him.

Just to make a complete eejit of himself, Apprentice John concluded by saying: 'Jack, you really didn't need to tell us that.'

Bradley laughed out loud. And Johnny joined in. He didn't know he could be that funny.

Photographs, detailed notes on all movements, personal inspection of the premises, the planting of bugs. Someone else would look after the phone tap.

I wasn't going to tell Bradley or Apprentice John that this kind of slow work makes me nervous, but it does. We had been issued with a tape recorder and a powerful directional microphone that would allow us to eavesdrop on conversations through windows and thin partitions. We had been given macro extensions that could be lowered down a chimney or an air-conditioning vent, or pushed under a door or through a keyhole. We were also issued with a similar piece of equipment for the covert gathering of video images.

The usual kit.

'It's tedious, I know,' Bradley said with a hint of sourness, 'but we need to be thorough.'

There was a heavy sigh from Apprentice John. He slouched back into his seat and cracked his knuckles.

'Harry . . .'

'Yes, Jack.'

'I want you to talk to that copper.' He pointed to a figure some way up the street.

No, Jack. We don't need to do this. What do you take me for? I'm past all that.

'The copper?'

'Yes. The copper.'

No fucking way. Send the apprentice.

'About the property?'

'Oh, I wouldn't ask about the house. That wouldn't be wise. Would it?'

'No. You want to know if he's married?'

Bradley shrugged. Apprentice John grinned until he met my glare. He too then shrugged.

Naturally, I was thinking I would stand with my back to Bradley and the apprentice while I asked the copper for some directions that didn't have him waving his arms about, then come back and lie.

But that wasn't an option because Bradley opened the glove compartment and took out a compact bugging kit that had a tiny lapel microphone.

'There you are. Put that on.'

I put it on, got out of the car and started across the road, suddenly feeling thoroughly depressed. There was a lot of traffic. While I lurched back and forth I tried to think of a credible approach.

Getting information out of a copper on the beat wasn't the same as getting information out of a lorry driver in a cafeteria. Bradley had really stuck it to me. Don't get annoyed, I thought. Concentrate on the task. Get the copper to talk in spite of Bradley.

Crossing the road I unintentionally walked into the path of a cyclist. She was a nervous woman with two rear-view mirrors mounted on her handlebars. She let out an alarming operatic trill, swerved erratically, first in one direction, then changed her mind and went in another. The flap of her coat smacked me on the chin as she passed. She maintained her speed as she continued down the street, but she was a tall woman on a tall bicycle and her centre of gravity was high. She continued to wobble spasmodically for some distance. She didn't look back.

The copper had seen it.

'Hoy, watch what you're doing,' he shouted.

'Yes. Sorry. I will.'

I made a short, chastened run on to the pavement.

'Bloody fool you are crossing the road like that. A danger to everybody.'

'Yes. You're right.'

I still hadn't worked out my approach. The near collision with the cyclist had thrown me and I couldn't find a way to turn the incident to my advantage. I just looked at the copper with my jaw locked. He had a mallet head and small, angry eyes set in shallow sockets, and that didn't help.

Come on, Harry. Talk.

'You want something, sir?'

Had I cornered him off duty in a pub there would have been a chance, but look at the way he was working those angry eyes under the rim of his peak. No-no. This was a waste of time.

'No . . .' I replied.

Because he had the peak of his helmet drawn down, his chin was up in the air. It had a bluish-purple hue. He had a perfect copper's shave. There was even a whiff of Old Spice aftershave.

'Nothing . . .' I said.

I reminded myself that in the field the agent is king. Fuck Bradley and his games.

I made a sensible withdrawal.

To begin with I said nothing when I got back into the car. I just took off the rig and handed it to Bradley.

'Thank you.'

'Any time.'

'A good call, Harry. No point in wasting time.'

'No.'

'Coppers . . . eh?'

'Yes.'

'I hate them, really,' Apprentice John added in a temperate voice. He was not trying to be helpful; he just wanted to convey that he had tried being reasonable with coppers in the past and it hadn't worked.

'Disappointing for you, all the same,' Bradley concluded, picking up on Johnny's mild tone.

It was then my turn to mimic.

'Yes. Very.'

Bradley gently cleared his throat and carefully returned the equipment to the glove compartment.

'Good sound out of that,' Apprentice John observed dully.

There was something about Bradley's appearance that was really annoying me that evening. It wasn't the ancient suit or the gorilla-stitched shoes. No – it was the pullover. The diameter of the neck was too small. It looked ridiculous over the shirt and tie. The expensive school pullover was his concession to going out on field work.

The more I looked at the second Adam's apple that was the tie knot under the pullover, the more annoyed I got.

'It's going to pay off,' he said. 'Now, here's a tenner for take-away coffees and scones.'

Scones . . . ?

He turned around in his seat and handed the money to Johnny. 'Get a receipt.'

He got out of the car with a flurry and made off down the street.

'Wanker,' declared Apprentice John without interest or conviction.

'Wanker,' I agreed wearily, and we both settled down easily to do our job.

The street had once been the principal thoroughfare of a quiet, affluent neighbourhood but it was now cluttered with small private hotels of varying standards. These were tall, narrow, thick-walled dwellings. Many of the cheaper hotels had replaced their single-glazed sash windows with plastic frames. The windows in our target house hadn't been touched and they rattled in their frames. The façade was in need of repair. A hundred and fifty years ago the batch of bricks used for this stretch of terrace had been baked at too high a temperature. Now, they were flaking; many of the bricks had lost their facings entirely.

There was a heavy front door that was a dull shade of royal blue. It had a mean letter-box that would polish up nicely, if anybody ever took the trouble. Beside the large bell push there were two wooden bases for brass plaques that had been removed some time before, judging by the near uniform discoloration of the wood.

We couldn't see the shallow roof from where we were, but it was reasonable to assume it was in a poor state of repair and would be dangerous to cross. There was a rusting metal brace that was fully supporting the chimney-stack. When this brace finally gave way, the heavy stack might plunge through all the floors to the basement.

Bradley hadn't told us much about who might be using the premises and for what purpose. We were to keep our eyes open for two men in particular coming and going at irregular hours. There were heavy curtains across the front windows, but the rooms were reasonably accessible. The panes of glass were large, and that suited us for our eavesdropping.

'We can get up on the roof, no bother,' Apprentice John observed. He was right. There were a number of points on the terrace where we might climb and make our way along. The route might be clear, but that didn't make the structure any safer. That had me worried and Johnny excited. 'We can see what it's like,' he continued happily. 'Probably all right if you go at it like a fairy. Basement access – one window with bars, one door . . . I'll check that.'

Because of the hotels there was a lot of traffic that would be unfamiliar to anyone watching from the house and that was an advantage.

'We should look again at the back,' I said. 'I'll do that.'

We set about our preliminary reconnaissance. I was confident that Apprentice John was more than able when it came to this kind of carry-on. He was a natural. He was like my copper friend Alfie, who knew the price of everything and the value of nothing. Johnny was a house-breaker who liked to be told what needed to be lifted.

We sat, we watched, we waited. After fetching water, surveillance must be the oldest assigned task known to man. Bradley hadn't told me if there was any connection between this job and the hunt that had ended with the death of our man in the suit. For now, I could only speculate.

During one of the long silences I looked at my hands that, oddly, were stuck to the steering wheel. They seemed to grow in size before my eyes. I decided that they had grown into the big hands of a French baker, but then I saw them for what they were – my father's hands growing on the end of my arms. The old man had told me once, quite out of the blue, that he had served entirely without distinction. He was looking at his hands when he told me this, and since then I had come to identify civil servants as having distinctive hands.

You get to make such observations on surveillance work.

Johnny and I got talking about partners, which, of course, can be a mistake. He got it into his head that my wife had just left me. That struck a chord with him. That set him off. He weighed in with a first aid diatribe which clearly he had just devised on the back of bitter personal experience.

'Right,' he said. 'She's done it. She's killed you. You and her are finished. *You* are finished. Whatever is left – that's you. That's the new self. The killed thing that's still walking the streets in your shoes and wearing your name. Have you noticed people look at you and say: there's another one? Have your friends been patting your green, scaly skin? Are they being patient with you? It's the way anyone would be with a corpse. You're killed. Maybe somebody you know has a sister who isn't too fussy. Good man. That's the spirit. Yes, but does she like Martians? Never worry. Somebody will see you right. Play your records. Read your books. Have a drink. Have a wank. You're dead.'

He was a reader. That was something in his favour. I told him that my wife and I hadn't been together for a long time, which wasn't altogether true. Then I told him how we first met. It was in a vegetarian restaurant.

'A good place for meeting women,' he interjected.

'I was recovering from a bout of food poisoning,' I told him. I wasn't vegetarian, I said.

'Most of them are skinny,' he added, but admitted to liking that.

'I caught her looking at me,' I told him. 'I think she decided she could trust a man with a book in his pocket.'

Now why did I volunteer these personal details? In our game there was good reason to be suspicious of an apprentice who was in his mid thirties. He had the wrong kind of sharpness if you were looking for insight. I was sure he had always been lacking in emotional ballast, depth of judgement and restraint. It wasn't difficult to see there was plenty of damage as a result.

'Do you miss her?' he asked. Perhaps he wasn't as sharp as I thought, nor I as inscrutable, because he ran on as though I had nodded my head. 'I mean, does she keep you awake? Sorry – don't answer that . . .'

I didn't answer.

'Who's she with now?' he continued. 'Some bloke who does novelty pancakes?'

He just couldn't hold back.

'The mind-reading at the end,' he said, 'that's the worst.'

I must have nodded again because he concluded with 'Don't think about it. Let it go', and a second, mumbled apology.

'What do you like to read?' I asked.

He shrugged, but it was an open shrug.

This time I was conscious of my nodding.

I knew Johnny was bursting to talk about himself but I didn't encourage it.

'It was only when they came looking for me that I fully realised how I was living,' he told me.

I think I was supposed to be impressed with his candidness. I was meant to draw him out.

'Really . . .' I said, and yawned. 'You were down in the South Seas somewhere, weren't you?'

'No.'

'Spain, then.'

'Not exactly.'

'Mexico.'

'No.'

I yawned again. 'I know it wasn't anywhere in South America. I just can't remember. You *did* mention it to me. I hardly know you.'

A terrible intimacy can be spawned on surveillance work. You have to watch out.

'Some villa belonging to a friend.' That I got right.

He began to describe a villa at the foot of a spectacular escarpment. A lovely place, he said. A beach three hundred yards away. At one end of this beach a rock locals called the 'Love Stone'; a nice whitewashed fishing village at the other. He told me that though it was a lovely place he lived in squalor. Got sunstroke because he fell asleep on the porch when he was drunk. That he fought with English lager louts in the village and screwed seventeen-year-old girls.

'Is your friend who owns the villa a criminal?' I asked.

'Oh yes,' he replied without hesitation. It was an expensive holiday home, he added.

The friend had also bought a second-hand bullet-proof car from a disgraced politician and businessman. It had fallen to Apprentice John to point out that although the glass was bulletproof, the door panels were not armour-plated and his criminal friend could have the bollix shot off him unless he were to wind down his window in a hurry and then, of course, he would get it in the head.

'What line of business is this friend in?' I asked, without any real interest.

'Tobacco.'

'Tobacco. Really . . . Then the car doesn't need to be absolutely bulletproof.'

Apprentice John said that obviously the car was for prestige and got us back on to the subject of his debauched exile. He parted his hair with the tips of the fingers of both hands to show me a small, white scar. 'See that . . .'

'I see it.'

'You know how I got that?'

'No. How did you get that, Johnny?'

'I was drunk and I climbed up this fucking windmill . . . one of those ones you see on the American plains, with a tail and a lot of blades . . .'

'You're in America now?'

'No. This is up the road from the villa.'

'Oh, I see.'

'I'm coming back from the village, right?'

'You've screwed some young girl and fought your way out . . . ?'

'And I climb up this fucking windmill . . .'

'Yes, I know about the windmill . . .'

'And I get this crack on the head.'

Christ, I thought – are we so bored that I have to listen to this? Apparently, we were.

'I still get headaches.' He described in detail now the moment the creature from the consulate found him living in squalor; how this public school shit found his way through the heat and the hazards of that natural splendour and stepped into the comfort of his friend's expensive villa to find our Johnny sprawled naked on the couch.

Was this a boast; some kind of false modesty? No. This was a lesson earnestly delivered. The best of us can slip. He and I would need to be on our guard. We would need to maintain high standards.

I had to laugh.

Then I stopped laughing and I struck my own cautionary note – 'So, you were hiding out with your friend and some manchild in the consulate knew where to find you?'

Johnny's face turned red and he shifted uneasily in his chair. 'I've stopped all that carry-on. I only drink wine with my dinner.'

'Glad to hear it.'

He still hadn't told me about his girl. Ignoring my own advice, I asked.

He started by telling me that his girlfriend had a hearing aid. It was a little plastic hernia in one ear. He told me it helped her to distinguish between background noise and sounds generated in the foreground. It meant that the damaged ear hardly hindered perspective. She never asked for anything to be repeated, he added. He said that her hearing was better than his or mine.

He didn't say anything more about the woman but, for some reason, thought I should have this fact about her having a hearing aid. I couldn't just leave it at that.

'Have you been seeing her long?'

He nodded.

'A sweet woman, yes?'

He nodded.

'How long has she had it – the hearing aid?'

'All her life,' he replied. 'You know anything about the human ear?'

'No.'

'Right then.'

I waited to hear about the human ear, but there were no more facts forthcoming.

'Tell me . . .'

'What?'

'Does she take it out when you're having sex?'

'It depends,' he said.

Mine was an impertinent question born of idle curiosity. I was surprised he gave me a straight answer.

'Fair enough.'

'Sometimes I take it out,' he continued.

'Oh . . . I see.'

'With my tongue.'

Well, he had me there. He wasn't making fun of me, but I felt foolish.

'You haven't told me her name.'

Reluctantly, he gave me her name. 'Tina.'

I could tell this was indeed the truth. I had just learned that Apprentice John was a poor liar when it came to personal matters.

It was only when I told Johnny that I was going to reconnoitre that I found I could let go of the steering wheel. It was dark. The street was relatively quiet. There had been no activity whatsoever in or about the house.

'Right,' I said, 'I'm doing it.'

'Right,' he said. 'I'll wait here.'

CHAPTER 8

I had twisted my ankle climbing up on the roof. It was nothing serious, but it was sore. I should have let Johnny do it. Now, I was trying to disguise the temporary limp. I called early. I thought I would catch her before she went out to work.

She opened the door smartly, as though she had been expecting a caller – and clearly, it wasn't me. Her body posture wasn't altogether unfriendly; her expression, however, was more of a challenge. She waited for me to speak.

'I see that eyebrow still works,' I said.

She gave me her weedkiller grin, which was nothing like her quick, engaging smile. Asking if I had called at an inconvenient time would have been a mistake, so I just gave her my even quicker, dependable smile.

'Come in,' she said. Her voice gave nothing away, which I took as encouraging. She extended the invitation, but she didn't move aside to let me in until I made a move.

I knew we belonged together by her smell. That came to me in a sudden and familiar rush as I touched the doorknob and brushed past her.

When she closed the door behind us I kissed her on the cheek. She surprised me by returning the kiss, but fully on the lips.

Her lips were dry. She'd been neglecting them, thinking about somebody else.

I wanted to root in her bag and get her lipstick and apply it to her lips. She bought expensive lipstick. It always made her lips moist.

But I couldn't go rooting in her bag. I couldn't touch her again without her leading, could I?

Her skin was tanned. It wasn't out of a bottle. She would never do that. Nor was it the work of a sunbed. The tan was lighter under the jawline. If she had had sunbed sessions she would have made sure to get a perfectly even tan. She had been on a holiday, and had spent more time walking than lying in the sun. Who had been on the holiday with her? Didn't she know I was still holding her hand?

'Harry,' she said for practice, to get the tone right in her own head.

She was less fearful now, I decided, but that might simply be because she was no longer with me.

So I touched her again, without her leading. I kissed her, this time on the mouth. I wanted to meet her halfway and then go an extra ten per cent.

'I can't keep away.'

I made the words sound playful, not desperate.

'You can, Harry.'

Distance doesn't always lend perspective. It can distort. The confidence I had accrued was suddenly in doubt. There was a yeasting-up of emotions that made the air between us thicker.

'You know you shouldn't just . . . arrive. You should have rung.'

'I know.'

I led the way to the kitchen.

'Do you want me to go?'

'No. Not yet.'

'You sure you don't have anything pressing? I can come back another time.'

'Nothing pressing.'

It's amazing the number of variations there are on nothing.

'Can I make some coffee?'

'Yes.'

'You'll have some?'

She hesitated. 'Yes. I will.'

She was studying me discreetly. She had always been discreet and I had always found that sexy in her.

I must have looked drawn and pale to her. An animal shaved of its fur.

'How are you?'

'How am I?' I repeated automatically. 'I'm fine. Things are going well.'

'Are they? I'm glad.'

What was it exactly that I wanted to drag out into the light?

'Very well, actually . . .'

I found the espresso pot. It was screwed together tightly. More tightly than I thought she could have done it. There were grounds in it, so I took it to the sink and rinsed it out.

I heard her silence behind me. I heard it beyond the sound of running water and my clumsy dismantling of the coffee pot.

'And you?'

'Yes,' she said. 'Good. I've been wondering about

you. You just disappear.' There was resignation rather than reproach in her voice.

I couldn't find the packet of coffee. She had a new place for it.

'There,' she said, pointing.

Her smell was getting stronger. I couldn't look at her directly. I could only glance at her. I would have to regain the initiative, and quickly.

'I see it,' I said, reaching.

But I put the packet down. I turned to her, put my hands on her hips and forced myself to look deeply into her eyes.

I thought the eyebrow might rise, but it didn't. She didn't move. She just left my hands on her hips, and that was a deadener.

I could let my hands slide off her hips, or I could snap them away and be businesslike about it. I snapped them away and threw them at the cupboards.

'Any biscuits?'

She got biscuits out of a cupboard where she used to keep tinned goods.

'Are you in trouble?' she asked.

'No. Definitely not.'

Was she going to compliment me on being good in a tight spot? That would have made me truly sad. I was a cautious man who had learned to take risks. The skill that got me out of tight spots didn't stretch beyond the survival mode. There was a failure of imagination. An undertaker with a screwdriver in his pocket was better equipped than me.

I was thinking that whatever she said, her voice would tell me what I needed to know, even if it were reduced to the leanest answer to the sharpest question.

I was mistaken.

She was paying a lot more attention to my questions than I was to her answers.

While I ate a biscuit I didn't want she suggested we should finally get the divorce proceedings over and done with.

I must have nodded in the affirmative because she nodded at me. Then something else came to her that suddenly engaged and entertained her.

'You're with somebody? You want to get married?'

'I'm with somebody,' I said, choking on a combination of my little lie and the biscuit crumbs, 'but it's still early days.'

For one mad moment I was borrowing Apprentice John's faraway sweetheart.

'Early days,' I said, 'but very nice.'

Was she going to blush? I thought she might. She blushed easily and that had a strong effect on me. Sometimes she would blush all the way down to her breasts and that would knock me on my heels.

'Well, that's good news, Harry.'

The boiling water had forced its way up from the lower chamber through the coffee grounds. It seemed to have happened very fast. Perhaps I hadn't put enough water in it.

She put out two cups with saucers and I poured quickly.

'It's not Ruth you're seeing?'

'No,' I replied. She must have seen my evasive eyes, for she followed up immediately.

'You've always liked her.'

'There was nothing between us,' I lied. It was barely a lie. 'I don't know why you think . . .'

I didn't get to finish.

'I mean, since Alfie's disappearance. You haven't been to see her?'

'I saw a lot of her at the time,' I said, choosing to be deaf to her inference. 'I'm sure you know that. She is your friend, too.'

'Yes. I keep in touch. I'm not prying, you understand. I just hope you've kept in touch.'

'Yes. I've talked to her on the phone.'

'She thinks the world of you.'

'No, it's just that she knows Alfie and I were friends.'

'Were . . . ?'

'Are. Of course, I mean, are.'

'You give up so easily sometimes, Harry.'

'You think so?'

'Ring Ruth. I know she'd like to talk to you.'

'I will.'

There was a measure of vanity in her scorn, but she was also satisfying a need to be daring. I could so easily dismiss her vigilance and her sharpness as the over-assertiveness of a woman who felt she was losing her looks.

I stretched the skin on my chin, made a show of my dead man's whiskers, and once again I was a fool radiant with hope.

False hope.

My visit was a mistake, I decided. I would have to leave. In a hurry.

With ease and informality she asked about my work with the firm and, with the same ease – or was it lack of interest? – accepted my clumsy attempt at vague answers. In spite of my best efforts she had noticed my limp, but had passed no comment.

Then, formally, she said: 'I should tell you, I'm seeing someone you know.'

I wanted to tell her that I was aware of that fact, but I didn't want her to think that I had been watching her; that I had been sneaky. So I continued to be sneaky.

'Jack Bradley,' she said.

'You have this all wrong,' I wanted to say. 'We were better together than either of us could have imagined.'

But the words dived back down my throat and dissolved in a sour mess in my stomach.

She read my face. 'You know, don't you?' It was a new relationship. She was wondering if Jack was indiscreet.

I let her wonder. It was the least I could do. But now I had to find something to say to prevent me from throwing up. The reality of their relationship was harder to take standing alone with her than watching the two of them together.

'It's none of my business.'

'You're right. It really has nothing to do with you and me, Harry.'

'Hey, it happens all the time.'

I couldn't hold out any longer. I made my way to the hall door. In the hall I turned abruptly to see if I might glimpse any weakness in her resolve.

There was none that I could detect. She spread my ribs and kissed my pig's heart.

*   *   *

You could call it shift work, but the roster could – and did – change without much warning. Johnny and I could find ourselves working two or more shifts in a row. We had to do it without complaining. On my way to the job one evening I got a call from the nursing home to tell me that there was a problem with Cecil. Could I come over as soon as possible?

'A problem . . . ?'

'Nothing medical, you understand,' said the matron. 'Your father is in good health.'

'He's been drinking?'

'Well, it's just that he won't co-operate.'

'He has – he's been drinking. What's he done?'

'He's sitting outside. He won't come in. We *have* tried. We won't force him. He's upset, Mr Fielding, but he won't tell us why and he won't budge. Perhaps you could come and see him now?'

'How much has he drunk? He's not a big drinker. A little could set him off.'

'He's really quite calm, Mr Fielding. I think he just needs to talk to the right person.'

I had to make a quick visit. Apprentice John covered for me. He stayed in the car and I took a taxi. It was raining heavily by the time I got there. As the taxi turned in through the gate I could see him sitting on an isolated bench overlooking the rose garden. A young nurse, one he liked, was sitting beside him holding an umbrella over the both of them.

I got the driver to park a little way past him, and then I called to him as I approached.

'Hello, Da,' I shouted in an upbeat voice. I rarely

addressed him so. When I talked to him I usually called him by his given name, if I used any form of address at all. He looked in my direction, but made no response other than to allow a flicker of recognition in the eyes. As I drew closer I could see that he was actually sitting on his hands.

He seemed to have set his features against all elements. He was determined not to speak.

The nurse responded with a big smile for me. Her concern for my old man was genuine, and so was her relief at my arrival. 'Hello, Mr Fielding. What an evening. Cecil – it's your son. Come inside and you two can have a cup of tea. You can have something stronger, if you like. I won't tell.'

There was no response. The rain beat down on the umbrella and pummelled the ground. I had thrown on my coat but already my ankles and my shoes were sodden.

'Where's your hat?' I asked him. I was a little concerned, but not surprised, to see that he had his pyjamas on under his heavy coat. He was wearing his heavy shoes with thick socks. 'You don't see many men wearing hats these days,' I said to the nurse. 'A hat looks good on Cecil. He likes to warm it on the television set.'

I sat down on the other side of him.

'Come on, Cecil,' the nurse said in a winning voice and with a squeeze of the old man's arm. 'Come inside.'

He turned to her slowly and looked at her with what seemed to be uncomprehending eyes. She returned a gentle, quizzical look.

'I'll go and get Matron,' she said, signalling to me that she would give me a chance to talk to him. 'Do you want me to look for your hat, Cecil?' she asked. He shook his head slowly. We were grateful for some response.

The nurse passed the umbrella to me, then made a dash for the entrance, where two other nurses were keeping vigil. I imagined they had tried shifting him by collectively showering him with attention and that had failed. Only the favourite had been allowed to stay with the umbrella.

When I had positioned the umbrella so that it gave the best shelter to both of us I linked arms with him. I had never done anything like that before. He accepted my self-conscious move as a natural comfort. I knew then that he was in great distress.

It was getting dark. The rain was getting heavier. Together, my father and I stared out across the black flower-beds to the trees at the boundary wall, our attention drawn by the impressive sound the pellets of rain were making as they drummed on the leaves.

We had sat together on the same bench before with the sun shining. We had gazed at old women in head scarfs seated in chairs on the lawn. I had observed a nurse covering the reddening feet of an old man in sandals I knew only as Jenkins. Jenkins got a special pot of tea. He got it before everyone else got theirs because he rose especially early each morning, my father had informed me as he took out a pair of nail scissors from his top pocket to open a bag of boiled sweets. Jenkins wore sunglasses you would expect to see on a racing driver or stunt pilot.

On a night like this Jenkins would be safely tucked up in bed. The noise of the rain in the trees would send him to sleep and he would dream of India or a cricket match on the green.

I decided that I should come at Cecil from an oblique angle. I would make him talk. I would raise a subject that would get his goat – my aunt Kate, with whom, against his better judgement, he was in love. Mention of his sister-in-law would make his blood pressure rise in a steep curve.

'Aunt Kate tells me she was in visiting you yesterday . . .'

He nodded. She had travelled from Dublin and made her own way to the home.

'Did she have the transistor radio in her handbag switched on? She does that deliberately, don't you think?'

No response.

'If she does, she carries it off brilliantly. She tells me the cheapest places for batteries are the sex shops . . .'

There was a faint smile. He was blinking repeatedly now.

'You don't think she buys batteries in sex shops, do you?'

He nodded, indicating that he did and that he was mildly disgusted.

'It's good that she's come over to visit . . . I know you're happy to see her . . . She's helping me with the house . . .'

He looked at me and I could see immediately the anxiety rise in him.

'Do nothing with my house,' he pleaded. The words

didn't sound right. Then I saw that he had a broken front tooth.

I asked him what had happened. He wouldn't say, at first. His teeth had always been a source of pride to him and now this broken tooth was causing him so much distress that he was attempting to ignore it completely. He asked me again what I was doing with his house. The house was another point of pride, though he had only camped in it since the death of my mother.

'Kate is helping me get it in order,' I said evasively. 'It needs work.'

'Kate,' he repeated, his attention suddenly redoubled.

'Yes. She showed up. Unannounced, of course.'

'Of course she did.'

I had to sell the house to keep him in the nursing home. Financially, it was the only way I could ensure he would be well looked after. He needed care now. He was past being able to live on his own. I couldn't say this to him. It would be too cruel a blow to inflict directly.

I looked at him. The damage altered his face more than I could reconcile with a missing third of a front tooth. I saw him struggling to suppress his anxiety. He was aware of his vulnerable position and was now afraid that his broken tooth would show him up to be an incompetent old fool who could not be trusted to look out for himself.

My heart went out to him. I needed to know what had happened. Had he fallen?

'Cecil,' I said, 'we're going to get that fixed. Tell me what happened.'

His chin sank slowly. The rain seemed to drum more loudly on the umbrella. Then, suddenly, he lifted his head and turned again to me directly and told me that he had broken the tooth drinking from a naggin of whiskey. Somehow, he had misjudged throwing back the contents and had struck the tooth with the mouth of the bottle. It had happened after Kate had left.

'You'll make an appointment with the dentist for me, will you?' he asked, abruptly rising to his feet.

'Of course I will,' I replied, springing to my feet, trying to keep us both covered.

'Come in with me,' he said.

'I will.'

'Kate didn't say anything about the house. Tell me about my house.'

CHAPTER 9

Bradley had told us there was a relief team with whom we were not to make contact. We were to stick to a rigid schedule. We were thinking the others were very good, because we hadn't spotted them. Did they think the same about us? I had my doubts.

I was very much later than I'd thought I would be. I blamed my twisted ankle.

'Anything?' I asked.

'Nothing.'

'Did you see the Georges?'

'No.'

'You look a wreck.'

'Thanks.'

We sat in the car. We watched. We waited.

A half an hour or more passed without either of us saying a word. I wondered when Bradley would call me in for debriefing. He didn't seem very interested. When I had come back from my ankle-twisting reconnoitre to describe the barren interior of the house, Apprentice John had also shown little interest. He had proceeded to describe a club he had visited where there was a gentleman whose job it was to wash your hands for you in the luxurious toilet. I needed to take my mind off the old man, so I took him up on his story.

And where was this club, anyway?

This club was in Spain.

Where in Spain?

In Barcelona.

A gay club, with tea dances and such?

Absolutely not.

And was this man there for you when you were taking a piss?

No. The washing came after.

Bereft of conversation, I decided I would ask Johnny about the incident that had led to his being fired from the job training volunteer aid workers.

Apprentice John had taken his shoes off. He had left them at attention on the floor. He had his legs drawn up to his chest and his heels on the seat. He was perched like a hawk in a tree, watching intently. If those shoes were to suddenly take off and attempt to fly out the car window, he'd be down on them instantly.

I took a run at the subject of his dismissal.

'So, you've always been a blowhard.'

'How do you mean?' He hadn't been called that before and he didn't like it. I suspect to his ears the word sounded altogether too tame – an indulgent term that might be used to describe a public school bully – and that would really annoy him.

'When things aren't going right you like a shouting match and a punch-up, if it can be managed.'

'Where's that coming from?'

'I was just thinking . . .'

'Were you now – thinking about what?'

'You never know what to do in a peaceful place. You drink and get sunburnt.'

'What are you on about?'

His neck had got longer. That was a good sign.

'I was thinking about you and the volunteer aid workers.'

'What about them?'

'You getting fired for being a blowhard, then taking off to Spain and getting drunk and sunburnt.'

The neck was fully extended now, the arms were folded and the chin was sticking out.

'Go on. Tell me what happened.'

He sighed heavily. He released enough tension in his muscles to allow himself to slide into a kind of rictus sprawl on the fusty cushion he had brought for the car seat.

'It was a lesson.'

'I know it was a lesson. What happened?'

'It wasn't just to show them what it might be like to meet some butcher in half a uniform. The job was to make it real. Put them under pressure.'

I was going to lead him. I was going to get him to admit to being a blowhard. Show me that he had learned something himself.

'You were getting them to read the situation? To negotiate?'

'I was forcing them to make decisions.'

'So you beat up one of them because he froze?'

'No.'

'That's what I heard.'

'Two of them.'

'You beat up two of them?'

'And they got that wrong, too. They got all fucking huffy and indignant. So I beat them some more.'

'So you laid into them?'

'*And* I smacked another one who fancied he was some kind of referee and thought he'd step in with a "now look here". Smacked him good and hard.'

'I take it you were playing the role of the militiaman?'

'Yes, Harry, I was. And you know those guys.'

'I do.'

'So I produced an automatic and I put it to one of these fuckers' heads.'

'After you beat him about the place?'

'After I beat the two of them and smacked the referee. They didn't know about the pistol. They thought I might use a finger or a wooden spoon.'

'You're going to tell me it wasn't loaded.'

'I took it away from his head and fired a blank.'

'Where was your supervisor?'

'Now you're sounding like these volunteers.'

'You were teaching them your way while the supervisor was on his tea break?'

'Not my way, Harry. The way of the butcher militiaman.'

'You didn't stop at any point to enlighten your students?'

'I did not.'

'You got carried away.'

He shook his head and gave another sigh. 'They weren't reading the situation, these three. They didn't appeal to my ego or to my military vanity. They didn't remind me what it was to be a good soldier. They didn't show respect for my rank. They didn't look into my eyes. They were going to let me get away with murder. Would you or I go into the jungle with these three? Fuck no.'

'Wait a minute. You haven't given me the scenario. What was the situation they were presented with?'

I had adopted one of Johnny's slouches, now. I was enjoying myself. I threw a foot up on the dashboard of the car. Apprentice John felt he should match my slovenliness and slid down further in the driver's seat. He put his open hands behind his head.

'There were other volunteers watching,' he said. 'They were the refugees. I suppose one or two of them might have learned something about saving lives.'

'Put me in the picture.'

'We had a bus. They were on the bus. Three of them escorting refugees through a region where there are no clear front-line positions in the war between the Blue people and the Green people. "You've seen other bus convoys moving through this region," they've been told. "These transport men and boys to the killing fields. Reports have it that the civilian bus drivers have been forced to put a bullet in one passenger's head at the end of their first run, so they won't be talking to anybody about these charters, either."'

'Blue people killing Green?'

'Yes. These are Blue buses with Green people. There may be Green buses with Blue refugees, but that's not today's news.'

'And your aid workers are escorting –?'

'Green refugees.'

'And they get stopped?'

'We drove them to an empty airbase hangar and shut the doors behind them.'

'And that's where you were waiting for them? Captain Baldhead and his gang of militia woolly-backs?'

'Correct. And our aid workers have to negotiate safe passage with me, Captain Baldhead, and they don't know which side I'm on. Now, as you can see, I'm not bald. But then the Blue people aren't blue and the Green people aren't green. Not on the outside. On the outside they all look the same. The volunteers are told this just before we turn into the air base.'

'First task for our workers is to keep their people on the bus, right?'

'Right,' I said.

'So, I order them off the bus.'

'And your workers respectfully but firmly refuse to allow it.'

'They do. And I start to barrack them. I spit on the Red Cross credentials one of them presents to me. I take their short wave radio. They hadn't thought to update their supervisor on the radio when they turned into the air base and now they want to make a call, but I don't let them. They sit back down in their seats. I get one of my woolly-backs to put in a window with an iron bar.'

'You actually get one of them to smash in a window of the bus?'

'Fucking right, I do. I want them off.'

'How do they react to this?'

'They get a fright, don't they. They're picking glass from down the back of their necks. It isn't cricket, is it?'

'So, what do they do?'

'One of them, she asks for my name. I'm happy

to give them my name. They still don't know which side I'm on. I ask her to identify the colour of her passengers. She tells me they are mixed. I laugh. She begins to quote military conventions.'

'And the other aid workers, they have said nothing so far?'

'That's the only thing they got right. They let one do the talking to begin with.'

'So, she's quoting conventions . . .'

'And then I tell her I will order my men to set fire to the bus if they don't get off immediately.'

'So, she decides to take her people off?'

'They get in a huddle. I can see they disagree, but she leads them all off the bus. I have the refugees line up against the bus facing my militia butcher boys.'

'And that's when the other three start causing trouble? That's when you lay into them?'

'No. I inspect the line. I walk slowly. The one with her hair done up in a pineapple, the one doing the talking so far, she's quite good. She walks with me. I sniff one of the refugees. I ask another if she knows where her husband is fighting. She doesn't know, of course.

'The one with the pineapple – she's almost got it right. But almost isn't good enough, is it, Harry?'

'Not in these circumstances.'

'Correct. She's kept calm. She's talking to me in a quiet, even voice and she's looking into my eyes. But she lets one of her co-workers get up on his high horse. She lets him quote more conventions about refugees. I don't like the tone of his voice and she knows it, but she lets him continue with his conventions. "Poetry in the mouths of villains," I tell him.'

'And that's when the others pipe up. That's when you start beating the living daylights out of them?'

'No. That's when I turn to the line of refugees and I say: "Blue people, two paces forward."'

I had been rotating my foot on the end of the leg – the damaged one, the one that wasn't up on the dashboard – while taking in his story. When he reached the part about the line-up and Blue people to step forward, the rotating stopped. I looked hard at Apprentice John.

'Life and death, Harry,' he said. 'Life and death.'

'Did anybody step forward?'

'They looked to each other, up and down the line. They looked to their protectors. This time, I shouted: "Blue, two paces forward."'

'And the three pipe up?'

'No. They started moving about in tight little circles, pulling at their faces. What are they going to do, Harry? You step forward and you might be saved or you might be doomed. There's going to be some killing.'

'What are they saying?'

'They're talking about saving civilians on both sides. About good works. The woman is signalling to the line that nobody is to step forward.'

'You shout again, right? Last warning. You're going to kill them all?'

'I am. And then one of these three workers goes to my militiamen and tells them they can't do this thing. Big mistake. That's when the three get huffy. That's when there's a bit of beating. That's when I take out the automatic and fire the blank. Hell of a sound in the hangar.'

'And you thought you'd get away with all of this?'

'I was in the moment.'

'You were in the moment?'

'Yes.'

'Oh, well then . . .'

'Be here now. Ever hear that phrase? I think it was John Lennon who said that. You should know. Your generation.'

'You think John Lennon would have beaten the aid workers then fired the automatic?'

'Harry,' he said, 'I'm an angry Buddhist.'

CHAPTER 10

The National Audit Office was dumping filing cabinets when we drove past the service entrance on our way to report to Bradley. Breaking into a solicitor's office or a government department to photograph or steal a few files out of a cabinet was rapidly becoming a thing of the past, and I didn't have the aptitude for snatching information out of cyberspace. I wondered how long it would be before I was compromised by this new handicap.

Bradley chose to meet us in a pizzeria on Cromwell Road. He had rung me on the mobile phone he had issued me, and called us in from our watch. He was on his way somewhere fancy and this place was convenient. We were running a little late. When we arrived he was waiting there with his coat on over formal attire. He looked pointedly at his watch.

'I suppose you spotted the relief team and had a little chat?' he asked Johnny.

'Oh, aye. We spotted them, all right.'

Johnny ordered pizza and I ordered spaghetti, then I reported on the surveillance and my illegal snooping.

'So it's empty?'

'Virtually,' I replied.

He got me to describe my journey through the house, room by room. He wanted to know what exactly there was in each room, though I had made it clear there was virtually no furniture, just a single iron bed in one. An old book on otherwise bare shelves in another, and a square, brass travel clock on the mantelpiece in the front living room.

'Carpets?'

'In all the rooms, except the kitchen, of course.'

'Bedclothes on the bed?'

'Yes.'

'No bedside lamp?'

'No.'

'And the clock, was it working?'

'No. It was stopped at five minutes to five. The alarm hand was fixed at five-thirty.'

'A.m. or p.m.?'

'No way of telling.'

'And the book?'

'Goldsmith's *History of the Earth and Animated Nature*.'

I thought I was doing very well. Was he going to ask for a publication date?

'Anything else?'

'Besides the bed, the travel clock and the book?'

'Yes,' he barked impatiently.

'A little pile of nail clippings on the draining board in the kitchen. A full set, if I remember.' I thought I'd get that in; whether or not he asked for a publication date for the book, I was sure he would want a count on these. 'And a half-eaten bowl of cornflakes with a spoon in it on top of the cistern in the bathroom,' I added. 'Judging by the mould, I'd say it's been there for several weeks.'

He was in a hurry. He had half a melted ice cream

in a dessert bowl in front of him. The spoon was face down on it at a perfect right angle, to indicate that he was finished.

'Tell me how you went about getting in.'

I described my route via the roof of the return, up on to the main roof and in through a skylight.

'What other possibilities were there?'

I gave an account of several approaches but stressed that the route I had chosen was undoubtedly the best.

'Good,' he said. He tossed a bunch of keys on the table. 'If anybody is breaking in you'll know which way they've come.'

'Sorry . . . ?'

'You heard me.'

It took a moment for it to sink in. Bradley was already up on his feet, and Apprentice John was grinning uncontrollably. Bradley soon wiped that off his face.

'There was no relief team, Johnny. Don't lie to me again.' He slipped two twenties and a tenner out of his wallet and handed them to Apprentice John, who was now feeling properly stupid. 'Here's fifty quid. We're expecting guests. I want you to buy cleaning fluids and some cloths and give the place a good clean. Top to bottom.' He turned to leave, then turned back again and indicated the money that was still folded in Johnny's hand. 'And you can pay for your dinners out of that.'

On the way out to visit the old man I asked myself if the nail clippings belonged to Bradley.

But you never get an answer to a question like that.

'What's the matter?' I asked the old man. He was looking at me with a curious cast.

'You need a good feed of liver,' he replied. 'I'm sure I'm not the only one to notice.' He was trying to give me something that he wanted to keep to himself. His concern for his own flesh and blood.

He asked about my wife.

How many times would I have to tell him that we had separated? And would he take in that I was about to win her back? He had asked about her many times now and the answer had always been the same. She was busy. She was asking for him.

He was prepared to accept that so much time could pass without her visiting, and that upset me.

'And how is she?'

'She's fine. She's working hard.'

'Good.'

'She's asking for you,' I said again.

He nodded with satisfaction and I nodded back. I hadn't told her about Cecil's move to the home. I was being selfish. I was afraid she might think I was looking for attention. I couldn't bear her pity.

He made some reference to the body's capacity for self-healing but stressed that a healthy liver was essential, and that liver fed liver. This was so obvious, he claimed, as to be incontrovertible. He then switched to talking about my work. My new job.

'I'm making big changes,' I told him. I was telling him again. I must have got it into my head that he needed to hear important information twice or more.

'A new job?'

'Yes.'

'You're doing the civil service exam?'

An informed guess on his part, but no.

'They're taking me in.'

He knew who I meant.

'Ah – that lot. They're tin gods in there, Harold. Remember, tin gods to a man.'

'I will. I'll remember.'

'I know you will. You have a good memory, and you're thorough. They like that.'

He asked about pay. I told him what I was earning.

'Does that include extras?' His civil service tone was coming through: the professional dryness; the stoic acceptance; the slightly jaded reasonableness in matters of money.

'No.'

'I should think not.' The same slightly jaded reasonableness.

He recommended that I should join the civil service pension scheme and suggested that if I was going to fiddle my expenses – something I knew he had never done – I should be damn smart about it. I could be sure there was a department snoop. 'Some bright young pup', as he put it.

'That car,' he wanted to know, 'is it laid on?'

I said that it was.

'Wait two months,' he advised, 'then get them to change it. You can do better.'

I said that I would.

'You can always dicker with the engine, you know – the bally thing keeps giving trouble, you say.'

'Cecil . . .'

'It's a nice car, but I'm sure you'll want something

a bit faster. Something with a bit more gizz. You can always put a few concrete blocks in the boot to keep it on the ground if you have to throw it around a corner. The comrades in the KGB used to do that with their Zils.'

Was he mocking? He didn't normally talk like this. I think he felt he should entertain me, so he kept talking.

'No civil service exam, then, no?'

'No.'

'A vocational appointment.'

'Something like that. There was a medical. And I got fitted for a suit.'

He snorted. I knew the idea of my visiting the tailor would amuse him.

'You'll have a shiny arse in a month. Don't go to any tailor they give you. They'll only let you have the cheap stuff. I know a better one. I'll pay the difference. In fact, I'll pay the lot. The Fielding males have always been well turned out.'

He gave me the name of a tailor in Savile Row.

'No exam, eah . . .' he said. Nothing could be judged from his tone, and that takes considerable skill.

I thought there was some pride in my achievement, some secret pleasure in my unorthodox induction that touched his scruff button, but I could only speculate.

There was a brief pause, then he said mischievously: 'They're not hiring you as an assassin, are they?'

He had another piece of advice for me. 'These tin gods, Harold. Remember, when they don't know, they don't know that they don't know. Do you follow?'

'I follow.'

'Good,' he said emphatically, and his spirits seemed to lift instantly. 'I knew you would.'

We went outside and a new mood took hold of him.

'Sorry about all of this,' he said, his shaky features for once set. He was referring to his getting old. 'Shouldn't be visited upon you, but there you are . . .' he said. 'And I count myself lucky,' he added directly.

He was making a formal declaration with these words. There was a resignation in his tone that carried no self-pity but rather seemed to suggest that if a person truly knew how lucky he was then he would be at liberty to take that good fortune for granted.

I saw that he would continue to make his plans for when he was well and able to leave and I colluded willingly. Was he deceiving me, I wondered? Was he trying to spare me? These plans were modest in ambition. They might just have been realisable a year or two earlier. To get on the tube and walk through a favourite section of Kew Gardens. To drive to France to visit an old friend. To go to the soap baths with his cronies and afterwards get drunk and stay awake.

There could be no comfortable way of living with himself unless he was in control. That was why he marvelled at the seamless repair to his broken tooth. The fixed tooth had given him new hope.

He would continue to do his exercise on the sloping path in the grounds of the nursing home. With the tip of his tongue pressed firmly against his marvellous new tooth he attacked the rise with more resolve than ever. Though he felt the need to apologise to me for his indigence, there would be no slacking on his part. He would fight the prospect that this physical exertion was an end in itself. It would, instead, be an integral part of his plan.

Humiliation was a feature of the job. Learning respect the hard way. It bothered Johnny less than it bothered me, but I kept that to myself. Bradley had been playing with us. Teaching us a lesson lest we get ideas above our station. The house he had us watch was an MI5 safe house that was being made available for an entrapment operation planned against Target A. There was likely to be some delay before Target A could be lured into that trap, the details of which we were not yet given. Johnny and I were to be ready to be called upon at very short notice, though our role in the operation was still to be defined. Everybody was to be patient.

Separately, but with the same vagueness, Apprentice John and I would come to learn that our lives were dedicated to recovery; getting back what each of us had lost.

For now, the closest either of us could get to recovering anything was an earnest attempt at making sense of what it was we did. To put a frame around it. Give it structure. Call it having a job. Call it a fresh start. Fresh ran contrary to vague, and that could only be a good thing.

We were in the house, looking over the place. I was helping him decide what he could get away with in terms of cleaning. Anything to take my mind off my personal problems.

'Are you going to marry Tina?' I asked.

He replied by telling me that she had asked the same question.

'"Are we going to get married?" she asked me.

'"No," I said.

'She didn't ask why not, so I told her it was because of her having a hearing aid.'

Was he serious? I couldn't tell. He was damaged enough to think like that.

'No handicaps when it comes to marriage, that's a policy with you, is it?'

'She laughed,' he said.

'Good. I'm glad to hear it. Do you spend much time with her?'

'I sit with her a lot. It's nice, just sitting.'

I wasn't getting the tone of this conversation at all. There was a failure to connect here. Apprentice John was inspecting the travel clock while he composed bad poetry.

'What . . . You sit and watch the telly?'

'We sit in parks, on buses, in the car, in her old man's garden. I was sitting with her and her old man in his garden the other day. He was talking about trees and I was looking at his daughter.'

'It must have made you nervous, having him there.'

'No. It didn't. Tina was just a little embarrassed and that really turned me on, and I liked hearing about the trees. I was enjoying waiting for her to smile back at me, waiting for her to blush. It was perfect.'

I tried to show appreciation with a nod. I knew that such moments of reverie existed, and that they were forceful and endured. Now I had the clock in my hand. The word EMPIRE was printed on its face in capital letters. It weighed heavy in the hand. It was old. Probably 1940s. It had been presented to somebody. There was a services emblem on the top. RMS *CARINTHIA*.

I put it down again on the mantelpiece.

'I think you should marry Tina.'

He grinned. 'We don't do it,' he said.

'You don't do it – how do you mean? You mean there's no sex?'

'There is, so far as it goes.'

'Wait a minute – are you telling me there's no –'

'No,' he replied, jumping in. 'Not yet.'

'And you've been seeing her for how long?'

'For a while,' he replied uneasily.

'You've been seeing her a long while, right?'

'I have.'

Beyond his immediate unease he seemed resigned to suffer some brand of exquisite torture.

'Ah, Johnny . . .'

'I know. Weird, isn't it?'

He was grinning again.

'Are we going to spend that fifty quid on cleaning fluids, or what?' This was the fifty quid that was well and truly spent.

He moved to the window and looked out.

'Imagine when we do, though,' he said. He wasn't talking about the fifty.

'You've seen her recently?' I asked.

'I have.'

'That's good then, isn't it?'

'Yes.'

'And she's well?'

'Yes.'

'And that's good too, then.'

'Yes. It is.'

'It went well . . . the evening?'

'Oh yes.'

'Did she hum in the bathroom?'

'How do you mean?'

'Was there humming after you did it?'

He was annoyed with himself for letting me ask impertinent questions about him and Tina, but he wanted to show that he wasn't fazed by my probing. He wanted me to be impressed by his stoicism, which I was.

'We didn't do it.'

'Oh.'

We were walking out to the hall at this point.

'What's this about humming?'

'It's a good sign, that's all.'

'When we do it, she'll hum.'

In my imagined scenario Johnny would sponge her down in the bath before finally making love to his far-away girlfriend, and there would be a lot of singing. In the morning, alone in the bathroom, she would hum to herself.

I could see he was getting annoyed with me.

'Johnny,' I said. 'When we come back, you get rid of the mouldy cornflakes and the nail clippings. I'll wind the clock.'

CHAPTER 11

We had had a few drinks. We were looking for the car when we heard the thud of leather boot on skull. It was coming from a lane just behind us. A van with its doors open blocked our line of sight. Johnny squatted to investigate.

'Never a policeman when you need one,' he said. He managed to make his words ring with sincerity.

'No, Johnny,' I said, catching his arm as he rose to his feet. 'Not our business.' This was my new sense of responsibility coming through. A more selective response that was to do with duty, that wasn't entirely me.

'Come on, Harry,' he said, moving sideways.

'No,' I called after him in a forced whisper, but my feet followed and my stomach turned over. 'Look, I'm the experienced one here . . .' I added stupidly.

'Right, then. Nothing bad is going to happen, is it?'

'Christ.'

I was never one for fist fights and this was taking an unnecessary risk.

They weren't gangsters as such. More like football hooligans or National Front thugs. In any case, they didn't recognise an angry Buddhist when they saw one. Apprentice John saw the challenge and didn't hesitate.

He went into animal alert mode. He advanced swiftly in stop-start movements.

There were four of them, each taking his turn to kick hell out of a fifth man who was doubled on the ground. They had driven their van down the lane and stopped at an angle. They had left the doors open to obscure the event. The driver had put on his flashing hazard lights, which was thoughtful of him.

Apprentice John got a better view of the beating. He waited for me to catch up.

He held his hand out without glancing in my direction. His gaze was locked on the action beyond the van.

'Give me the gun,' he said in a low, even voice.

'Are you mad?'

'Gimme.'

'Not a chance.'

'Harry, do you want me to get hurt? Give me the gun.'

I gave him the automatic. I slipped it to him efficiently. Got it into his hand in the right position in one quick move. What the hell was I doing that for?

He put the gun in his pocket and walked up to the driver's side of the van. The driver was just getting out – he wanted to get in his share of the kicking. He was a young, handsome boy with a tanned and polished shaved head.

Apprentice John caught him full force on the jaw with a roundhouse kick as he turned.

The blow sent the boy reeling back into the van

to collapse in an unconscious state. I think he bit his tongue. Apprentice John was past the van and in the arena they had created in an instant.

The man being beaten was in a bad way. His brown skin was torn over both cheek-bones. He was wearing a T-shirt that was half ripped from his torso. There was a lot of blood pumping from a wound through which two broken ribs were protruding.

'I hate it when they don't show a bit of fight,' Apprentice John said breezily as the attackers turned to react to the disturbance behind them.

I came up on the other side, slamming the front passenger door as I passed. One of the three came forward and took out a knife. The other two followed. They were tough and weren't a bit afraid.

'Are you any good with that?' Apprentice John asked without slowing his advance.

'Oh yeah.'

We could tell by the way he handled himself that that was the truth, and the other two were happy to leave the stabbing and the slashing to their pal. They were looking forward to a demonstration of his gutting skills.

'I'm good with a knife, but I don't have mine with me, do I, George?' Johnny said, turning to me.

'No, George. You don't.'

I could see this was going to get out of hand and there would be no restraining Apprentice John. When he moved to face them side on I saw him take a quick glance left and right, and I began to panic.

'No, George,' I repeated, but with a very different emphasis.

Johnny went ahead regardless.

'I'm not so good with this,' he said, effortlessly pulling out the automatic, releasing the safety catch and putting a bullet in the chamber. 'I need to be real close to be sure.'

He raised the gun. The muzzle was three feet from our hero's eyeball, which rapidly dilated to take in as much information as possible. The information was unambiguous.

'How quick are you?' Johnny asked. 'I sometimes hesitate.'

These thugs knew enough to read that glance left and right and they could see that Apprentice John was nicely wound. All three froze.

The young Asian on the ground moaned, turned over on his belly and began to crawl up the brick wall by his bloody fingertips. Johnny wasn't at all interested in him.

The knife was still in the hand in front of him. He made our new friend lower it just by looking at it. When the beaten man collapsed back into a heap on the ground I went to his aid.

'Come on, George,' I said to Apprentice John. 'Time for tea.'

'All right, then,' Johnny replied brightly and struck our friend across the jaw with the butt of the gun, which was a very dangerous act with the safety catch off. The blow knocked our man back into the arms of his friends and sent the knife scudding across the ground.

Apprentice John turned abruptly and walked away.

'Hey,' I called after him, 'aren't you going to give me a hand here?' This Asian boy with whom I was slow dancing was half dead.

The injured driver was coming to and attempting to climb out of the van.

'With you now,' Johnny called back. He swung the door on its hinges and batted the driver back inside.

The two thugs still standing lunged at me and, in the very short time that elapsed before Apprentice John could intervene, delivered a series of heavy blows.

But then Johnny got to work.

There was somebody watching now from the far end of the lane. Another shaved head, but this one was a Tibetan monk in an overcoat several sizes too big for him. He stood there, flat-footed. A fold of his robe showed under the coat when he raised a hand and sang or chanted something.

In any case, his presence prevented Apprentice John from discharging the gun.

The whole business was an absolute disgrace. When Johnny turned his twinkling eyes on me again and saw the expression on my face, he said: 'Hey, I'm making trouble. I'm happy.'

There must have been a full moon above the blanket of cloud because they were all out that night – the hooligans, the down-and-outs, slightly drunk MI5 employees.

'Excuse me, young man,' the skinniest of the down-and-outs said, approaching Johnny as he fumbled for the keys to the car. When I heard the voice, it was so polite I thought it belonged to the monk; but he had vanished.

The vagrant was wearing a thick woollen pullover that was once white over a grubby striped shirt. Both collar wings of the shirt were pointing to the sky. 'You're in a hurry, but excuse me, by the way.'

No. We weren't in a hurry. I was getting a headache, Johnny hadn't come down. He was still elated.

This one wasn't drunk or aggressive. I put my hand in my pocket and produced what change I had. Four pound coins and two twopenny pieces.

'Is it that bloody obvious?' he asked.

'Never mind,' I said, giving him the coins. 'On you go.'

'Things haven't been going well at all,' he said. The emphasis was on 'at all', but with a strain of gentle self-mocking.

'I know the feeling,' I said. He acknowledged this as a truth.

I shouldn't have taken the money out of my pocket so quickly. I should have shown more respect and let him speak first.

He looked at the coins. 'Good man,' he said. 'On you go. On you go.' He wished me well and told me that he was in a hurry too. He put his hands in the trouser pockets of an old brown suit and moved away. Evidently, he wasn't quite used to walking in the gleaming pair of cheap white runners that were on his feet.

'Christ,' said Johnny, 'that was an easy few quid he got.'

I thought about Bradley and my ex-wife together. This kind of humiliation didn't lead to respect. Winning her back, that was what I had to concentrate on. On the way to see the old man I talked to her the way I talk to dead friends when I'm alone and driving the car.

But she wasn't listening.

'Stop that,' I said to the old man. 'Stop pretending you're unhappy.'

He was in the hall, dressed in his pyjamas and slippers. He was eating an egg mashed with breadcrumbs and butter in a cup. I knew there was butter because it was dribbling down his chin.

He looked at me blankly. There was a beat. Then he farted.

'Eggs,' he said.

'Eggs,' I echoed lamely.

'I like an egg.'

'I know you do.'

'You want to walk?' He had got in the habit of thinking I was coming to him for counsel and I didn't discourage him. And, I suppose, in a way it was true, though I had made no request for such.

He moved ahead of me down the corridor.

'You want to stay inside,' I called after him.

He turned impatiently. 'I'm not staying stuck in here.' There was another, shorter beat while he quickly came to realise that he would have to put on his shoes, his trousers and his coat.

Coming back down the corridor to the staircase he managed a brief, wry smile.

'I expect I'd be happier with some clothes on.'

'You would.'

He handed me the cup with the remains of the mashed egg. 'You ditch that. I've had enough.'

He told me he would be back shortly, and went upstairs.

I had just put the cup down on a table beside a vase filled with large plastic flowers, when the matron addressed me.

'Mr Fielding, may I have a word?'

My experience with this question is that you can only reply in the affirmative or seek to delay by responding with some variation on 'not now, I'm busy, but later'. 'No, you may not have a word' is rarely an option.

'Eh, well, I *am* in rather a hurry.' I was far too polite for my own good.

'Just a minute of your time.'

I turned to face her square on and struck a kind of military at-ease stance that let her know I was indeed a busy man and invited her to get to the point immediately.

'It's about your father . . .' She was signalling tolerance with a formal note of reluctance.

'He's been acting up, has he?'

'Well, he has been singing.'

'Singing?' Cecil singing – that surprised me. 'What – singing loudly?'

'Singing with no clothes on.'

'Singing in the pelt? Singing loudly with no clothes on . . . in public?'

'Well, he tends to start in the lavatory.'

'And then he comes out stripped?'

I just couldn't see it. Was he cracking up?

'You see, he goes to the lavatory for privacy. So that he can drink spirits.'

'Ah hah.'

'And really, it's not permitted. The drinking, I mean. You understand.'

'I certainly do.'

'Good. So, we understand each other.'

'We certainly do.' She wanted me to admonish the old man. She wanted the supply stopped.

'Very good.'

'Nothing more need be said on the matter, then.'

I wanted to ask what songs Cecil was singing. What songs did he know? I could only remember him singing in the car on the way to the beach when I was a child. Matron was now signalling that she was quite sure nothing more needed to be said.

I thanked her and went upstairs to his room, where I found him moping.

'You've been singing.'

'Yes,' he admitted weightily.

'At the top of your voice.'

'Singing to myself,' he insisted. 'Certainly not for anybody else in here.'

'No singing if you want to drink.'

'Christ on a bike.'

'They've caught you because you didn't keep your mouth shut. Now, that isn't like you, Cecil. Locking yourself in the toilet and getting drunk – really, has it come to that?'

'I'm enjoying myself,' he said bitterly.

I let a moment pass.

'This is a good place,' I said.

'I know it is,' he replied quickly. He looked away, and suddenly the whole business was breaking my heart.

'What songs do you sing?'

Now, he was embarrassed as well as upset.

'Oh . . . this and that . . .'

'No singing in the toilet if you want to drink. Go outside or sing when you're not drinking. And another thing – keep your clothes on. Did you tell them I was bringing in the whiskey?'

'Of course not.'

'Good. I know you're discreet, and we have to be discreet if I'm to keep you supplied.'

It was an absurd conversation and that was what saved us.

'Now, look,' I said, producing a flat bottle from my pocket, 'that'll keep you going but remember, they're on to you.'

'Right.'

'I'll try to get in more often, but it's difficult at the moment.'

'Right.'

'It's working out?'

'It is. Will we walk? Or would you like some of this?' He held out the bottle. 'If you have the time we could go for a drive. I'd rather we had a drink in a pub.'

He was fretting because he felt I could easily lose interest. He felt that he should entertain me.

'Hide that,' I said, smacking the bottle with my palm, 'and get your coat. I'll tell them you're coming out with me.'

'Right.'

Though it did not register in his characteristically inscrutable response, I knew he was greatly relieved that we would have a little more time together.

We went to the day room for tea. Kate was going to make another visit soon, I told him.

'Always too busy to come and see us,' he said. 'Rachel always makes excuses, of course.' He was referring to my long-dead mother.

I didn't see immediately the significance of the comment being delivered in the present tense, but it didn't take long.

'What does your mother say this time?' he asked.

I didn't make a direct response. I told him again that Aunt Kate would be making another visit.

Then he asked why hadn't my mother visited him? He was embarrassed that she should come to see him in such a place, but he was missing her terribly.

I didn't know what to say. I watched him put a small cloud of milk in his tea.

Something had collapsed. Something had given way and he had lost an entire stratum of memory. The reality of a death had been undone.

When I told him that she was dead it was as if he were receiving the news for the first time.

'I'm sorry,' I said. I was already in free fall.

'What happened, Harold?' The blood was draining from his face.

'She died a long time ago,' I said. I thought it would make it easier if I wasn't specific.

'No . . .' he said quietly. I could see his heart was struggling to pump blood to his head. He swayed a little. I put a hand on his arm.

'We both know she's gone, Da,' I said.

He rallied quickly. It took the form of a rising panic, which was infectious.

'Dead,' he said. I could see him struggling to recognise that this was a fact he should grasp above all other facts. 'Oh, Christ.'

'We know she's gone, Da,' I repeated.

'It should be me,' he said. 'She's so young. She's dead? Rachel is dead? Yes. She is. Of course she is.'

He was frightened and ashamed that he had forgotten this truth. He put three fingers into his scalding cup of tea.

As quickly as he had plunged them into the hot liquid I removed them. I played it as though it had just been a mistake. A cup of tea put in the wrong place.

'Now,' I said, without looking at the three fingers, 'there's no point in telling Kate not to come and visit because she'll come anyway. Correct?'

'Yes.'

'Good. I'm glad that's straight.'

'Where is she?'

'She's in Dublin, but she's coming over just as soon as she can. I'll collect her from the airport.'

'Where's your mother?'

'She's in Temple Hill,' I told him. 'The Quaker cemetery in Dublin.'

He was looking at me hard now. He didn't want any evasiveness.

'You were there?'

By that I took him to mean I was at her funeral.

'We were all there,' I said.

'Yes,' he acknowledged. He took his hard gaze away slowly to search the middle distance. I glanced at his three scalded fingers. They were red, but there was no blistering.

'Come on, Cecil,' I said, springing to my feet, 'let's go out in the garden.'

He responded quickly, as people in shock sometimes do. He rose to his feet and gave an emphatic nod. 'Yes. We should do that.'

'Are you all right?' I asked.

'Yes, I'm all right,' he replied.

He practised the meagre language of pain with a cursory grunt as he momentarily held out his three red fingers. The gesture was meant to address his great loss. 'I'm a bloody fool,' he declared, but not unkindly.

CHAPTER 12

'You have the place clean and tidy?' Bradley asked.

We hadn't lifted a finger, but Johnny replied that we had 'given it a good going-over'.

'I'm glad,' said Bradley, 'because you're both moving in temporarily.'

And so I gathered some of my things from the Camden kip I had been living in and brought them to the house in Pimlico. I made sure I got the bed. A few sticks of furniture had miraculously appeared, but there was only one bed. Apprentice John got some petty cash and bought a camp bed which he put in a large bedroom at the back.

There was an old cheerlessness about the interior that had little to do with the design, or the pre-vailing light. Nor was it much to do with the state of the structure, but rather was the result of some other abstruse neglect. Nothing very bad had happened here. With a bit of imagination a retard or a lowly employee of the firm might think it big enough to make a world if they could get a few friends to call.

The first night there I found that Johnny had lined up the nail clippings on the draining board in something like the appropriate order for a pair of feet. He had cleared away the mouldy cornflakes, and had washed and dried the bowl and spoon. They were on the draining board beside the nail clippings.

While I brooded over personal strategies he read from Goldsmith's *History of the Earth and Animated Nature*. He was engrossed and had, for the moment, forgotten that ours was quickly shaping up to being a miserable existence.

'Chapter on animals . . . right?'

'Oh yes . . .'

'"A Comparison of Animals with the Inferior Ranks of Creation,"' he quoted.

'I see . . .'

'It says here: "The vegetable, which is fixed to one spot, and obliged to wait for its accidental supplies of nourishment, may be considered as the prisoner of nature. Unable to correct the disadvantages of its situation, or shield itself from the dangers that surround it . . ."'

'There's no such thing as nature, Johnny. There's only trees, and plants and animals . . .'

'What are you talking about?'

'Wind and rain and sunshine . . .'

'What . . . ?'

'It's a theory.'

'Fucking reading about nature here.'

'Go ahead . . .'

'The vegetable . . . right, "every object that has motion may be its destroyer."'

'Stands to reason.'

'"But animals are endowed with powers of motion and defence. The greatest part are capable, by changing place, of commanding nature."' He was laying heavy emphasis on the word 'nature'.

'Pair of vegetables we are, sitting here, eah?'

'No, but listen, "Every animal, by some means or other, finds protection from injury; either from its force, or courage, its swiftness, or cunning. Some are protected by hiding in convenient places; and others by taking refuge in a hard resisting shell. But vegetables are totally unprotected; they are exposed to every assailant, and patiently submissive in every attack. In a word, an animal is an organized being that is in some measure provided for its own security; a vegetable is destitute of every protection."'

'What . . . ?' I said, holding out my hands wide, palms uppermost.

'It's good, though, isn't it? The way it's written. It makes you think. But we take it for granted.'

'What?' I repeated.

'That we can describe the difference between an animal and a vegetable.'

'Ah, now Johnny . . .'

'But when you read the likes of this you say, now here's somebody who can really explain.'

Apprentice John was a natural recruit; but he was also a troublemaker with the measured diffidence of a French waiter. In fact, there was something of the waiter about Johnny. He was expert at clearing space, tidying away, serving up.

You like that in a delinquent. It's a common trait among petty gangsters, lags and felons who don't have it in them to lead.

The first time Johnny offered to make tea and toast I watched him at work in the kitchen. He went at it quickly and efficiently. The extras were included.

He put sugar in a bowl. He wiped the teaspoon. He buttered the toast into the corners of my two slices as well as his own.

He brought it to our newly arrived table and served it up, but drank his own tea and ate his own toast standing. Afterwards, he washed the dishes and put them away with the same quickness.

'Thanks very much, Johnny,' I said, but Johnny offered no reply, just the slightest of waiterly nods. I tried again. 'I feel sorry for her.'

'Who?'

'Your friend, Tina.'

'Why are you sorry for her?'

'You being the way you are.'

'What's that supposed to mean?'

'You letting it go on the way you're doing.'

'Letting it go – no-no. You've got this wrong. I'm letting nothing go on. I'm showing a bit of respect. She likes that.'

'Winding yourself up.'

'I'm sorry I told you about her.'

'Wrong kind of encouragement, letting it go on like that.'

'I'm doing nicely, thank you.'

'Saving yourself – that's the new thing for you, is it? You should save some money and take her on a good holiday.'

He was right. What did I know about his affairs? I just didn't want him deluding himself as I had done in the past.

'You're laughing at me,' he protested.

'I'm not laughing.'

'You are, I can see it.'

'If I was laughing you'd see it.'

'Go ahead. Doesn't bother me.'

'Now you're annoying me.'

'Doesn't bother me at all.'

He asked if I had a photograph of my wife in my wallet. I did, and against my better judgement, I showed it to him.

Out of respect for me Apprentice John made a point of not being impressed with her, but I saw through that. 'It's the mind-reading,' he observed sometime later in the car.

'The what?'

'The mind-reading you're supposed to do,' he continued, in the matter-of-fact voice he had adopted for the subject. 'That's what gets you in the end.'

'With women?' I asked. I wanted to be sure I was following the right track.

'With women,' he confirmed. There was a pause, then he modified his matter-of-fact tone to something more introspective. 'They're never noble.'

'Never noble . . . ?' I was surprised.

'Wouldn't you agree?'

'I'll have to think about that.'

He fancied he was on a bit of a roll with his observations. 'Reason hasn't tapped you on the temple,' he said. 'Harry, you're a private person and I respect that, but my experience is that a private person is a patient person – often too patient. Do you hear me?'

'There's nothing tapping me on the temple.'

'It seems to me that you need to recognise that she's let you down.'

'Let me down?' I gasped in indignation. Then I realised he was leading me with his deliberate choice of a mild phrase.

'Betrayed you,' he added. 'Fucked you over.' He managed to make the tone of these steely words friendly, not malicious. He was, after all, trying to reassure me.

He was grinning at me. The grin seemed to suggest that one private, patient man could measure his suffering against another's well-being.

And that was unsettling.

'We're running late,' I said.

'Now that she's dumped you she'll not have a word said against you. Funny, isn't it?'

His words were more prophetic than he could have imagined. You see, I knew that Bradley was having an affair with her. Screwing her, I could say.

'I'm up to speed on this one, Harry. I'm with you.'

'You're with me . . . ?'

'On your side. Completely. Goes without saying.'

In the Service you demonstrate loyalty; you don't speak of it if you know what's good for you. Otherwise, people might get the wrong idea. They might think you are giving others the same line. You start to look a little too sincere. I would have to have a word with Apprentice John to make sure that he understood this. I made a mental note. I didn't want to lecture him on the point that day. I was feeling a bit tender myself.

'Thank you, John.'

We passed a fat man in a raincoat sitting in a parked car. He was eating half a cooked chicken from his lap. Grease running down the backs of his hands glistened in a burst of sunlight. An ambulance sped past, its siren blaring. He carried on regardless, and so did we.

Bradley had given us a brief. Call him Target B. There was a connection with Target A. He was a first secretary in his country's embassy. He felt comfortable among the old women with chickens' necks, botched face-lifts, rinsed hair that was coiffed up over their balding crowns. Then there were the younger Arab women. More Arab women frequented these Mayfair casinos than Arab men. He especially liked to flirt with these women. He liked to think he could seduce any one of them, or every one of them in time.

We watched him. You could see it in the way he walked among them giving his favourites his subtle signal. He was ripe for exploitation.

Nothing much happened for him that first night. He went home early. Johnny was very disappointed. He thought I was, too.

'Are you still annoyed with me over the thugs?'

'Yes.'

'Well, that's all right. It's your wife, though, isn't it? She's preying on your mind?'

'No.'

'Harry,' he said, 'I'm going to help you.'

'Are you?' Now why did my heart sink, sitting in that car with him in Mayfair?

'Yes, I am.'

I didn't want to know, but I asked. 'And how will you do that?'

'I'll get you thinking straight.'

'Will you, now?'

'Yes. I will.'

I should have known better. I *did* know better. 'Go on, then.'

'Now that's a good start – wanting to move ahead.'

I should be able to see whatever it is that's coming, I thought, but I couldn't. He had caught me at a weak moment.

'And what's your approach, to women, like?' he asked.

I just looked at him blankly.

'They give up on me,' I said with a cheeriness that belied the blankness. 'That's my game.'

As if I had an all-embracing strategy. As if I needed to impress him with my wardrobe of shiny armour.

He turned over the engine, pulled out at full lock, swung back straight and took off up the street. He made a call on the mobile to arrange something social with a couple of girls as we drove to another club.

He was full of easy talk on the phone. To my ears he sounded like an overconfident teenager. There were two women at the other end of the line. They took turns talking to Johnny.

The windscreen wipers slashed back and forth. Apprentice John laughed as easily as he talked. I stared out at the mix of shiny and blotchy shapes strung along the wet pavements.

The place was cluttered with tables covered with old linen cloths that were far too long. Each table had a cheap Christmas candle burning in a clumsy metal holder with a dragon motif. You could buy a long ton of that metal gear in India for the change in your pockets.

'What do you think?' Johnny said, barely containing his own enthusiasm for the place.

'I'd say if you drank out of the wrong glass here you'd wake up in Shanghai with a beard.'

He took that as favourable comment on his choice of recreational spots.

There weren't many people present, but still, it seemed quite full. There was a pianist playing standards and singing into a cave located somewhere deep in his imagination. The owner and manager, a tall, one-quarter black woman with an attractive voice, was whiffled. She was trying to encourage a family atmosphere.

She had a child sitting on a stool in a corner at the end of the bar. It was well past her daughter's bedtime but the girl seemed used to the set-up. There was a pile of shopping bags around the legs of the stool. For one reason or another the lift home from the shopping trip hadn't materialised.

The owner welcomed Johnny with an unsteady hug, and a bottle of wine, compliments of the house. It was just after midnight when we sat down at one of the doll's house tables with our free bottle of wine and two cloudy glasses. I began to relax, to surrender myself to the night. I picked out a woman across the room. The more I watched her the more I was attracted to her, and she saw this and deflected my attention with a determined look.

Then this fool entered and joined the party and her face lit up. The ignition was a brief flash of anger which almost immediately melted away. Obviously, he was inexcusably late. He had a bottle of spirits in each of his two jacket pockets which seemed to act as ballast.

He greeted her and began to dance around her. He wasn't about to explain himself, though he did offer her a cheeky leer. He danced with a hunch – a giant in a small space. He glanced up at her repeatedly and with each glance the beaming response he had first elicited was renewed.

His dancing took him in my direction. He smelled of whiskey and sweat and vaguely of piss, but she didn't care. Perhaps she was even spurred by it. In any case, she had forgotten that he had stood her up.

Now he was beaming at her in short bursts without missing a beat of his monkey stamp and she was moving closer to him, dancing with a smooth roll of her slender hips.

At the bar beside the tired but precocious girl and her mother there was an irregular with a face that had the smoothness and consistency of his ear lobes. He was turned out in the clothes of a well-to-do barrister, but he also wore ill-fitting glasses to confirm his status as fully fledged misfit. He had taken off his very expensive watch and had it propped on the counter in front of him. He was swaying slightly because he had had a lot to drink. He was also trying hard to find a comfortable posture. It was obvious that children made him nervous.

The girl made faces at him and gave him two fingers. He tried to engage rather than ignore her and just made himself more uncomfortable because the mother didn't like the look of him either.

He nodded enthusiastically at Johnny and gave a big smile. Johnny nodded back and gave a friendly salute.

'You know him well, do you?'

'Lovely man.'

'Alcoholic barrister.'

'They're trained to it. He likes the marching powder, too.'

He was nodding at me, now. Evidently, any friend of Johnny's was a friend of his.

'Very friendly,' I said.

'He likes me. He thinks I'm a bigger crook than him.'

On the other side of the barrister there was what looked like a honeymoon couple, and, beside them, two women ordering double gins. In a dark corner beyond the bar there was a knot of people who, quite possibly, had been there for several days undisturbed, generating a lot of three-quarter-speed laughter and coils of dirty blue smoke.

We were settling in at the cramped bar when a heavy-set guy seemed to step through the wall. He came over to us and addressed Johnny.

'Don't I know you?' he said, moving in from the side and leaving his mouth open.

I knew that Apprentice John had seen him earlier ballooning among the crowd, looking in our direction, but had chosen not to initiate a connection. The approach had a clumsy discretion to it.

'No,' replied Johnny.

'I do,' said the man. 'I know your brother-in-law, Francis. Know him well. Remember, the party at his flat? Can I buy you a drink?'

'No thanks,' said Johnny. 'We're both sorted.'

He was balding and had the appearance of a man in his late forties, but I suspected he was in his early thirties. He wore an expensive suit. He grinned. 'Johnny, isn't it?'

Johnny shrugged imprecisely, and that's a difficult thing to get right.

'Do you live around here?' His new friend felt he should ask. He was swaying a little. Not because he was drunk, for he was entirely sober, but to show that he was attentive.

'No,' replied Johnny. I suspected there were going to be a lot of 'no's, but still he managed to sound reasonably indulgent.

'I heard about the trouble . . . you know . . . your brother-in-law Francis . . .'

'Not my brother-in-law.'

'Well, whatever . . . your sister's boyfriend.'

'Trouble? What kind of trouble?'

'In the police station.'

'Yes . . . ?'

'In Victoria . . . I see Francis occasionally . . .'

'You do . . . ?'

'Of course I wouldn't be saying a word to anyone.'

'No . . .' There was a downward inflection in Johnny's tone that seemed to indicate an absolute faith in the man's discretion.

'It's good that it's sorted . . .'

'Yes.' The 'no's were turning into 'yes'es, but they were deadeners none the less.

'I'm getting you a drink. And your friend here . . . ?'

'I'll have a Black Bush,' I said.

He was relieved that I spoke up, and Johnny was irritated. I thought I'd press the situation a little further. After all, we were both bored. 'Johnny's a rude scut for not introducing us. And your name is?'

He immediately apologised, said his name was Paul Gleason and put out a big, soft hand for me to shake. I shook it vigorously and gave him my name.

He had committed himself now so he bravely took Johnny's hand and made him shake on the belated introduction.

I was enjoying myself. Johnny was concentrating hard on strategy and suppressing what would undoubtedly turn into a cold rage should he not get the upper hand.

'Did you hear about the trouble down below?' he said, underplaying beautifully with a little turn of the head.

'No,' replied Paul, dropping his voice, the same clumsy discretion at work.

'Ah well . . .' said Johnny, pretending to lose interest immediately. Even I felt I should play along. I took a precautionary glance over his shoulder.

Paul Gleason was suddenly thrown. He desperately wanted to be accepted. 'I'm saying nothing,' he assured us both. He hailed the bartender and pointed to our glasses. 'Same again for these gentlemen.'

'Aren't you having one?' I asked.

'No-no. I'll not be interrupting. I just wanted to say hello.'

'That's all right, Paul,' Johnny said solemnly.

'Family stuff . . . down below, John, yes?' He didn't

know what 'down below' meant and couldn't resist asking.

Johnny gave another of his ambiguous shrugs. He had the upper hand now and Paul Gleason, stuck for words, was shuffling from one foot to the other waiting for the two drinks to arrive.

Johnny repeated his ambiguous shrug, which suggested that an appropriate response was called for.

Paul let go with some verbal diarrhoea.

'I have a fleet of vans. No job too small – or too big. If ever you need a van . . .' Blah, blah, blah.

Johnny tore a tiny corner of paper from a flyer that was on the counter. 'Write your name, address and telephone number on that,' he said. 'Land line, mobile and fax.'

Paul Gleason had to borrow a biro from the bartender. He was long-sighted and had trouble writing the information on the scrap of paper, but he persevered. He then had the privilege of lining up another round for Johnny and me before he shambled away.

'So, what was the trouble with your sister's boyfriend?' I asked.

It didn't take much for the cold rage to surface.

'He wasn't right for her.'

'Oh. I see. He wasn't treating her well?'

'I had to sort it.'

He wasn't giving much away. I decided I'd ask him about it another time.

'You were looking out for your sister,' I said, just to round things off.

'I was,' he replied. He made a concerted effort to change the subject and lower his blood pressure. The switch in his tone was impressive. 'You've got to keep your eye on the main chance,' he advised me happily as he poured more wine.

'The main chance . . .'

'The one goal.'

'Oh yes. Well, thank you for sharing that.'

'I've two perfectly lovely women here – no, *girls* – and you appear to be in another place.'

'No. I'm right here, Johnny.'

'You're in another place and that's pathetic given what I've organised for us.'

'I'm just tired.'

'Two lovely, lovely girls.'

'We'll have to make the most of the situation, then, won't we?'

'You're . . .' – for a moment he couldn't find the word – 'pining.'

'No. I'm not.'

'The main chance, Harry. I'm surprised I have to lecture you like this.'

He caught me glancing at the two women across the room.

'Are they looking at us?' he asked. 'I bet they're looking at us and they're feeling good about themselves. They have no problem with the main chance. You can tell that, can't you?'

'And what about this woman you've been telling me about?'

He gave a little impatient gasp, took me by the elbow and pulled me in close, partly to stop me staring at the two women, partly to give more dramatic emphasis to what was bound to be a leaky statement.

'I have to go through these situations to get there. Don't you see that?'

'No.' I didn't expect his justification to be quite that porous.

He glanced at the women, gave a big, reassuring smile, and quickly turned back to me.

'Harry,' he said, blinking, 'you have to move on, and I'm helping you do that.'

'Yes, but what about your friend – what's her name? Tina. Tina is the main chance in your case, right?'

The blinking hadn't stopped. In fact, it was intensifying. 'Now you're making fun of me.'

'No. I just want to know what *you* mean by the main chance. I have my priorities. I'm not confused, like you.'

'Look,' he said, stepping in closer still and blinking furiously now, 'you're pining for your wife and your wife isn't remotely interested in you any more, right? That's what you told me . . .'

I nodded. It started as a slow, less-than-committed nod, but I couldn't help it falling into some kind of synchronous rhythm with his blinking.

'Your wife is no longer the main chance, right? You're the one who's confused. I'm not confused. I *know* Tina is my main chance, but she's not in a position just now and that is why I can do this.' He gave a little flick of the head in the direction of the two women. 'Now *you* have to be looking for a new situation.'

'Sorry, Johnny, you're talking shite. And now they're coming over.'

He glanced again at the two women, who were

weaving their way towards us. Were it not for the whiplash gear they were wearing you might have thought Apprentice John was gazing appreciatively across some vast plain at a pair of Apache horses approaching at full gallop.

He beckoned to them encouragingly, as though they might otherwise shy away at the last moment, but really we both knew there was absolutely no prospect of that happening.

'You behave yourself,' he said, out of the side of his mouth. He beamed at them and they beamed back. They came right up close, pushing their bellies forward, which, I admit, was nice.

But then, Apprentice John froze.

'Don't move,' he said, putting his hands out and dropping his head. 'Stay right where you are.'

He went into a crouch, swung left and right, then got down on his hands and knees. 'I've lost a contact lens. Don't fucking move.'

We froze.

He wouldn't accept any assistance from the three of us. While Apprentice John gently brushed the sticky compacted carpet pile with the flats of his fingers I beamed at our guests as best I could, which was not very brightly.

'Haven't you got those disposable ones, then?' said the blonder of the two, addressing Johnny's hunched back. 'That would be a good idea for somebody like you.'

The other one was embarrassed by her friend's tactlessness and flushed in a rather attractive way.

Johnny wasn't in the least bit put out and soon he

surfaced with the tiny plastic dish on the end of an index finger.

'There,' he said, cleaned it on the tip of his tongue, and turned away briefly to insert it.

The blonde one seemed to be turned on by Johnny's lens-licking and wanted to see him put it in.

I positioned myself so that it was clear the quieter, flushed one was my date, and she seemed to like that. I had a picture of Apprentice John lying back with his hands behind his head, his contact lenses catching the light from a bare sixty-watt bulb in the ceiling. I could see him give a little nod in the direction of his groin and, as though referring to scraps on a plate, say: 'Here, are you eating that?'

I knew then that the night ahead would be a disaster. Harry Fielding wasn't up to it. In a short time he would be making a fool of himself in front of a stranger.

'Hello,' she said, smiling through her flush. There was a strong smell of drink on her breath.

'Hello,' I replied.

In spite of her shyness she asked me to look at her, so I did. Later she would ask me to lie on top of her and I would, with the same cement eyes.

The blonde one kissed Johnny on the cheek and asked, 'You boys ready, then?'

Johnny volunteered that we were indeed ready.

CHAPTER 13

My non-communicative brother and I talked the matter through after a fashion. We weighed the facts and came to a logical conclusion. The old man had broached the subject earlier with me himself. He was aware of his failing health and had swept aside my qualms with a wave of his hand. He had done so without hesitation. He was being brave.

We didn't want him ending his days in a land of metal soup bowls. He deserved better, and this was how we could ensure he would get a room to himself with the care that he needed.

'Sell it,' our father said. 'You must sell it.'

'It's the right thing to do,' I heard myself respond without thinking any further. 'The money goes straight into the bank in your name.'

There was another of his dismissive waves, and I felt worse about the whole business.

'Now, when you're ready to come out of here we can get you a nice flat. Something good, a place you can manage.' *Nice* was not a word I used often, but there it was, howling at me now that it was out in the open.

'I'd rather that,' he concurred. 'The house is getting me down.'

I told him that my brother was fully supportive of the move.

'Harold, if either of you think for a moment I'm moving in with him and his lot you've another think coming.'

I assured him that was never an option.

'Damn right, it's not,' he confirmed.

Of course he didn't want to be a burden. So, there I was with Apprentice John, both of us drunk, and me at the wheel of a hired van.

There was no driveway to my father's house in Muswell Hill. We had trouble finding a parking space anywhere near the gate.

'Recognise any of those cars?' Johnny asked. 'Any of them belong to neighbours?'

I recognised none of them. I drove around the block three times. I hadn't anticipated this simple problem. Pulling in anywhere where I could find a space and having another drink started to look like a solution. I was more upset by the whole business than I cared to admit.

'Right,' said Apprentice John as we approached the house for the fourth pass, 'stop.'

'Stop? Stop where? I can't stop.'

'Stop outside the gate. Stop in the middle of the road. I'll make enquiries.'

So I stopped. The traffic behind would have to negotiate the narrow space between the cars parked on the far side of the street and our big box van.

'What are you doing?' Johnny asked, calling back into the cab.

'What do you mean, what am I doing? I'm sitting here and letting you do something about getting me a space.'

'Are you mad? You'll only get abuse.'

I got out and went with Johnny. Angry drivers blew their horns. Apprentice John nodded reassuringly, indicating that the noise would only help our case.

'Do you know these people?' he asked me at the door of the immediate neighbours. The hall door flew open before I had time to answer.

'Good afternoon, Mrs Harvey,' I said, and Johnny made the same friendly greeting, even though he was a stranger.

'Mrs Harvey,' he said, butting in, 'Harry wants to talk to you . . .' I gave him a hard glare, then turned to her. I might have made some kind of a nodding motion, I'm not sure. '. . . But I need your help to clear a space for the van.' He pointed to the traffic jam that was rapidly building. 'As you can see, it's a bit of an emergency.'

She knew who owned the car parked directly across the street and we were able to get it moved. Johnny manoeuvred the van into the space while I trotted out platitudes to Mrs Harvey about Cecil's life in the home.

'It's for the best,' I assured her, but she didn't seem to agree. She would visit him soon, she told me, and added that his back garden was running wild. She claimed to have seen a rat. Her proposed visit, her reference to the overgrown garden and the phantom rat were all expressions of her scepticism.

'If there's one rat there's more,' she said, watching anxiously as Apprentice John raised a fiery finger to a disgruntled driver who, as yet, had not been able to pass.

Apprentice John caught us both watching him. He

stopped his aggressive strutting and stood for a moment in the middle of the road to give us a big, friendly wave.

'Why do they want *us*?' Johnny asked out of the blue. For him it was still a honeymoon period with the firm, and he was full of guileless curiosity.

'Let me ask you a question,' I replied. 'Which would you rather take hunting in the woods — a professor of animal behaviour or a dog?'

Johnny liked the idea that we were MI5 dogs. I kept my grave misgivings to myself.

We had the van packed with furniture and boxes of books, clothes and kitchen stuff. I let him do the driving. Ever the practical Johnny, he had suppressed his dislike of Paul Gleason, the doubtful friend of his sister's boyfriend, and got me a good deal on the van.

We had delivered two loads to my brother's house. This third load was going to a self-storage warehouse. There had been a brief rest and a couple of drinks between each trip. The more Apprentice John had to drink the heavier his head seemed to get. In consequence, his neck was getting shorter. His head was sinking into his torso and the wings of his car coat were rising around his ears.

Neither of us should have been driving, but moving house is a distressing business. I was the distressed one and he was being sympathetic.

'You swear on your mother's grave you're not holding back on me on the job? You swear you know nothing more than me?'

I swore.

'Yes, but the suits . . .'

God bless his innocence.

'We all have them, even the dogs. It's better than having to salute.'

'No shoes, you notice. Cheapskates.'

'Is there something wrong with the engine or is your driving getting worse?'

'What are you saying?'

'You think it's going to cut out? You're driving faster. You're getting careless. You make me think we can't rely on this van.'

'You're right. This is a heap.'

'Now you're talking like a bank robber. Slow down.'

He slowed down.

Then, he speeded up again. We came to a set of traffic lights which changed from red to green as we pulled up. The car in front was slow to start. Apprentice John gunned the accelerator.

'Come on, come on,' he shouted. 'Are you waiting for one particular shade of green?'

He was embarrassed, in case I thought he was easily duped when it came to motors. If that was the case, there were two of us.

He kept gunning the accelerator. Then, perversely, he delayed the traffic behind us while he gave the car in front a head start. He took off after it with a screech of tyres and overtook it in a reckless swerving manoeuvre, and instantly forgot about the matter.

'I'm putting in for a new pair of shoes,' he said.

Then, suddenly, we had a problem.

'There's only so many tests they can do on a piss,' Apprentice John said. 'What are they doing out there?'

If the effect of the alcohol had worn off, why did we feel the need to speak to each other in such a weighty, emphatic manner – that was what I was puzzling over.

'Look, I'm sorry about this,' I said. 'It's my fault.'

He shrugged. He was being unambiguously ambiguous.

'Let me do the talking.'

'All right,' he said. He may or may not have been aggrieved by my landing us in this mess, but he didn't seem too concerned about the immediate situation.

'You're familiar with these surroundings?' It was an insult of sorts. I was annoyed at my own ineptitude. Being upset at moving the old man's stuff out of the house wasn't a good enough excuse. I could have got drunk after the event. Anyway, in answer to my barbed question I got another shrug.

'You know what to expect?'

Apprentice John turned to me and, without rancour, declared: 'We both know these guys have no elastic in their knickers.'

I took this in for a moment, and then nodded. He was holding my gaze so I knew he was looking for confirmation. I also knew that he wouldn't leave the talking to me.

I had good reason to be annoyed with us both.

'They're trying to raise Bradley,' I said.

'And what do you think Bradley is doing? Fuck. Is he trying to raise Clements?'

'He'll not bother Clements. Clements will only get the hump.'

'I'm afraid to look down in case I see a pair of boy's legs in short pants. What's the delay?'

'It's the gun and the knife, Johnny, not the piss.'

'But we've explained . . .'

'You told each copper in turn to fuck off, that we were working for the Queen.'

'Yes, but you gave them Bradley's number. Bradley doesn't have to gather the fools into a circle over this, does he? He just tells them to let us go. I mean, show a bit of contempt. Show a bit of muscle.'

'You see, it's that kind of attitude that's keeping us here. That, and being drunk while driving a van.'

'And having the gun and the knife.'

'And having an automatic and a flick-knife.'

'I might as well be talking into a bucket as talking to you.'

'You were the one who was driving. Your driving got us into this. And you acting the tough guy got us searched.'

There could be no denying I was right on all counts.

'Maybe we should have got them to ring Clements,' he croaked belatedly.

'You have a number?'

'No.'

'You think he'd take a call from you?'

'No.'

He was being honest, not humble.

'Clements calls us, we don't call Clements.'

'I'd say you'd have to be good at explaining away absolutely anything to have his job.'

'He's the only one I know who can talk through his forehead. Believe me, you don't want him to know about you driving while under the influence, and you don't want to have any dealings with him. Too dangerous.'

Johnny scoffed. There was nothing he liked better than going behind God's back.

'I used to have a teacher in school like that,' he said.

'No you didn't.'

'I had a bit of a stammer when I was a kid and this teacher used to make me stand up and recite poetry. And I'd stammer. And he'd prompt me with his forehead. And when that didn't work – and it never worked, I just got mesmerised by a pimple in a sea of wrinkles on his fucking forehead – when that didn't work, he'd get angry and he'd mock me.'

'Please, Johnny . . . I don't want to hear.'

'So I told my dad, and my dad came to the school to have a word with Mr-fucking-Pimple. Mr Pimple tells him he's only trying to help me break my stammer. After all, a boy needs to be able to speak clearly. And my dad says – 'He can w-wr-write it down, can't he?''

Once again, I looked over at the door. I wasn't about to give any credence to Johnny's little discourse.

'Christ, what *are* they doing out there?' he demanded.

Three grinning Special Branch detectives came into the interview room. They were feeling smug and were determined to enjoy themselves. They took up various slouching positions and the grins disappeared in a professional manner. I thought I should seize the initiative.

'We need to be about our business.'

'Excuse me?' said the one who had elected to have his fun first.

'You heard.'

'I don't think you appreciate the seriousness of your situation.'

'Don't talk to these monkeys,' Apprentice John said, testing the smoothness of the bare wooden table in front of us with the palms of both hands.

One of the detectives raised himself out of his slouch, but really, none of them was much bothered.

'Is this an interview?' I asked.

'Oh, there's no interview being conducted here . . .' the detective replied soothingly.

'Monkey talk,' Apprentice John observed.

'If this is an interview you should switch on the tape machine.'

The detective turned to his colleagues. 'We don't interview members of the Security Service, do we?'

'No, we don't,' one replied with a smirk. 'Leave those boys alone, that's what we're told.'

'You've no idea how clever they are,' the third one added. 'Always on the job. Always after the villains we don't know about.'

'Monkeys,' Apprentice John said, in a private communication to me.

He wanted to goad them, but he wasn't being malicious. He had picked up the 'monkey' phrase from me recently. It was in common usage in the Service and was applied to the lowliest muscle men. He liked the sound of it, just as he liked the idea of being an MI5 dog. I made a mental note to reprimand him on his letting others see that he had an affinity with dogs and monkeys.

'I'm sure you've made the call,' I said, and repeated that we needed to be about our business.

'You have a car?' the detective asked.

'You know I have a car,' I replied. 'We've been through this.'

'And the registration is . . . ?'

I gave him the registration number.

'What colour is your car, Mr Fielding?'

'Dirty donkey colour.' Watch your own mouth, Harry, I thought. Watch the animal thing.

'You two share this car, do you?'

'I give him a lift.'

'To work?'

'Yes. To work.'

'Live together, do you?'

'No.'

'Not queers?'

'Well, how did you guess?'

'Don't mock, Harry. There'll be a full report.'

'You claim the furniture is your father's?' said another of the detectives. Something in his tone told me this was the one to watch.

'Yes.'

'Moving him, you say?'

'Yes. Moving him.'

'Selling the house?'

'Yes.'

'Get a good price for the house?'

'What's the delay?' Johnny asked. He was sitting on his anger, but the measure of it was beginning to show.

Our new interrogator turned slowly to Apprentice John.

'You were driving, weren't you?'

'You know I was driving.'

'Drunk.'

'They told you that?'

'Don't get smart with me. Cowboys, the pair of you. The back doors of the van were bloody well swinging on their hinges.'

'I've a question for you,' said Johnny. 'Will you ask the monkeys who followed us did they run over the foot spa.'

'You're determined to be smart, aren't you?'

'You know . . . The blue thing with the foot pads . . .' He indicated me with a jerk of the head. 'I think his da's foot spa fell out the back and those fucking monkeys ran over it.'

There was no reply because at that point the desk sergeant summoned the three detectives from the room, and, shortly after, Johnny and I were led from the interview room to the station desk.

'I'd sit down if I were you, gents,' the desk sergeant said. 'It'll be a while yet.'

'Is the van out the back?' I asked.

'Yes. It is.'

I asked him to make a call to the storage firm, to see if they would be open until six-thirty.

'You'll not be finished here in time for that,' I was told. 'The District Commissioner insists your master comes down here and sees the situation for himself.'

'What situation?'

'Apparently, your office doesn't know anything about any furniture being moved.' He glanced over his shoulder to a room with an open door where the three detectives were smoking around a desk. One was on the telephone and he was talking about us. It was a yes-sir, no-sir, three-bags-full-sir conversation, but all three of them were looking out at us and had the same stupid grin on their faces.

The desk sergeant went into mock-confidant mode. 'If you ask me it's to do with the drinking. The Commissioner is a stickler on drinking and driving.'

Johnny's eyes met mine and I shook my head wearily. I expect we both had a vision of Bradley coming through the door of the police station, circling us with a cocked snout, sniffing our breath. The prospect of getting on in the world suddenly didn't look so good. That was what I was thinking, but Apprentice John was too angry, too wound up in the moment to be bothered with the larger consequences.

When the telephone conversation was finished in the other room the quietest of the three came and stood in the doorway with his hands in his pockets and his head hanging to one side. 'You're being collected,' he said, as the others followed him out.

'See that box of radios,' Johnny said, indicating a cardboard box of police radio sets that was visible on the floor behind the sergeant's station, 'they're broken, aren't they?'

Neither the sergeant nor the others made any reply.

'They're broken,' Johnny assured me. 'They're being sent out to be fixed. It's not that they're faulty. You see, if these monkeys hit somebody over the head with their radio instead of their truncheon they don't have to fill out a report.'

This was the remark that caused the scuffle, and that surprised me.

Apprentice John had the detective on the ground in an instant and was ready to take on the other two and the desk sergeant when I pulled him aside and restrained him. Pacifying the copper on the ground was altogether another matter and required my knocking Johnny about a bit and pretending to give him a severe dressing-down.

CHAPTER 14

When the charges against us were promptly dropped, Apprentice John declared that we were, without the shadow of a doubt, fully inside the fold and had full-time, permanent jobs.

'You see,' he said, with another of his shrugs.

'No,' I said. 'I don't see.'

He thought I was being grumpy.

Bradley summoned me to his office for a private chat. He told me he hadn't bothered Clements with news of our serious breach of professional conduct. He said that he knew I had been under pressure; that moving my father into a home and having to sell the family house was stressful. I imagined Bradley in bed with my wife. The little chat was already making me sick and I hadn't yet opened my mouth.

He didn't want to lose me, he added. Didn't want me failing to measure up. Didn't want me turfed out on my ear. This job they had planned would prove my worth. Nothing was to get in the way of my proving myself; and our hothead, Johnny Weeks, was getting his chance, too.

He told me he never was one for taking on the clockwork cretins. He wasn't afraid of a bit of personality showing.

I counted the sailing ships painted on the shade of

his desk lamp. I thought he was going to rehearse his entire catalogue of ideological fixations, then caution me to be wise in moderation, that is to say, warn me that a man could get too smart for his own good. As it happened, I wasn't altogether wide of the mark.

'Mr Clements and I take different approaches,' he informed me. 'He likes to force evolution. I'm more of a stockbroker myself. I like to speculate. That's why I've taken the pair of you on, and that's why Mr Clements won't be hearing about this little incident. You see, I'd be pissing on his flower-bed if I told him, and, believe me, nobody with any sense does that.'

'No.'

'Any good stockbroker will tell you that investment is trade gone wrong, Harry. Business isn't getting done. I like to generate business.'

I nodded to indicate that all my close friends were good stockbrokers and had confided as much.

Actually, his little nugget of moderate wisdom got me going on another tack entirely; it got me thinking about Lollards, those fourteenth-century churchmen who, during the plague, took Church law into their own hands. Jack Bradley had trouble concealing his ambition. Our Jack likes a good plague, I was thinking, when he surprised me with a reference to my wife.

'By the way, I don't want you calling to the house unannounced. It isn't fair.'

He waited for a response.

I remained perfectly still. Perfectly dumb.

I saw that he too was motionless and dumb. And he was better at it than me.

'Thanks for being so understanding,' I said, referring

to the arrest. 'I have one more van load to move. Johnny and I will do that early tomorrow morning, if you don't mind.'

Target B, as it turned out, was Target A's brother-in-law. The task was simple enough. We had to put a case of wine in Target B's car boot without him or anybody else seeing us. Trivial though this act may appear, it was part of a serious scheme to discredit the man. Other aspects of the operation included tampering with his mail and depositing money in an account in his name. It was the firm's attempt to prompt Target B into making imprudent contact with his brother-in-law in order to set the record straight with his superiors. To tell him that he was the target of a smear campaign. The firm needed a traceable connection to Target A. There were other initiatives which had the same purpose. We could only assume that whatever was to happen in the safe house was part of one such operation.

Putting the wine in the boot of the car was work for fledglings, but Bradley was punishing us. Our indignity was copper-fastened by having to pay for the wine out of our own pockets. Naturally, we chose the cheapest wine we could get. Apprentice John got us a ten-per-cent discount in a backstreet off-licence where they seemed to know him.

Johnny and I felt our humiliation acutely.

The job was simple, but carrying it out was more difficult than you might imagine. Getting access to the car was not easy. The vehicle had diplomatic plates and was rarely left unattended, other than in the secure garage belonging to the embassy.

I was hesitant about the job. I was also smarting from the indignity of it all. The older I get the more difficult and, seemingly, the more dangerous the simple tasks appear. The greater the risk of failure.

I let Apprentice John lead on this one. Privately, I was thinking I might get back some of the street nerve that had been dulled by years of experience.

'Not a problem,' said Johnny.

'You know how we can do it without being dramatic?' I asked. 'I'd hate us to be dramatic.'

'Is this what we're going to be doing?' he wanted to know. 'Fucking stealing cars and buying drinks for third-rate diplomats.'

'It's a small job that needs to be done. That's all.' I didn't sound convincing and that annoyed him. He thought I was responsible for our disgrace. After the rush we had got from our display of arrogance at the police station, we were both feeling exposed.

'Are we off the big job?'

'Look, I'm sorry, all right.' His bad driving may have got us stopped, and his acting the tough guy had got us searched, but I wanted to acknowledge that he had been doing me a favour helping me clear out the old man's house.

'Nothing to be sorry about, Harry. I just asked are we off the big job?'

'Let's assume we're not.'

'Suits me.'

'So what's the plan,' I asked, 'with the case of plonk?'

'I cause a bit of trouble. You put the wine in the boot.'

As plans went it hardly inspired confidence.

'You have something worked out.'

'I will have.'

'Why does my heart sink?'

'Because you're getting old, Harry.'

'Drive the car, will you?'

We took off down the road to begin surveillance and identify our opportunity to deliver our gift.

Suddenly, I felt very tired.

'So, Harry,' he said, very happy with himself, 'you haven't told me what school was like for you. Was there any Mr Pimple in your life? There's always a Mr Pimple, right?'

'Do you remember *The Man from U.N.C.L.E.*?' I asked.

'I've seen it. Afternoon telly.'

'You've seen the reruns. I used to watch it as a kid. Thursday evening, after my tea.'

'And?'

'Fanatic, I was. Had the gun. Got my mother to buy me a black polo-neck.'

'*Star Trek* was more my thing.'

'United Network Command for Law and Enforcement.'

'American telly, eh . . .'

'You could send away for merchandise. I sent away. I got a badge, a membership card, a decoder, a pen with invisible ink.'

'Oh yeah?'

'Had my photograph taken in the back garden — me in the polo-neck, with my gun and my badge. Stuck the photograph in the membership card. NAME:

Harold Fielding. AGE: Nine and a half. COLOUR OF EYES: Brown.'

'You're eyes aren't brown.'

'I know. HEIGHT: Four foot six and three-quarter inches. WEIGHT: Four stone. Then opposite the photograph there was the declaration: I HEREBY DECLARE THAT *Harold Fielding* IS A FULLY-FLEDGED AGENT OF THE UNITED NETWORK COMMAND FOR LAW AND ENFORCEMENT AND MUST BE TREATED WITH THE RESPECT DUE TO ONE IN SUCH AN IMPORTANT POSITION.'

'Show your membership card to Bradley. He might learn something.'

'One day I did my homework in invisible ink.'

'Oh, very good.'

'You write in invisible ink and then you hold the paper close to a flame and up it comes – a light brown trace. It's water, lemon juice and a little pink dye, I think.'

'What did the teacher say? Full marks for imagination, yeah?'

'No. She thought I was messing. She thought I was making fun of her. You see, here's the point – she didn't know about invisible ink. She smoked but she wouldn't let me use her cigarette lighter. She wouldn't let me try putting it on the radiator.'

'Did you not show her your membership card?'

'You're missing the point. How could she be a teacher and not know about invisible ink? How could she expect to be treated with the respect due to one in such an important position when she didn't know about the ink?'

'Point taken.'

'How could the teacher not know, Johnny? That was a red-letter day for me.'

'And that's what has you here today, right?'

'Right,' I replied.

It was hell getting the wine into the boot of the car. We managed to do it two nights later. Johnny commented it was like something from a Laurel and Hardy film. No it wasn't. The lurking about, the false starts with the humping of the wine back and forth, and the fumbling with the boot lock had me feeling ill.

When that was done Bradley wanted to up the ante, and quickly. So we paid Target B another visit.

'Tell me,' Apprentice John said as, once again, we sat in the car across the street from the garage, 'why aren't you doing it?'

He was looking at the pistol Bradley had issued him for this one task. He had it resting in the palm of his hand, as though he were guessing its weight.

'I don't do that kind of thing unless I have to, and I don't have to.'

'And I do.'

'You're the apprentice. Besides, you like it.'

'Discharging a firearm in a public place,' he said mockingly. 'It's a serious business.'

'I hope you know what you're doing. I haven't seen you use that thing.'

This wasn't like Laurel and Hardy, he decided. It was more like a French farce.

I disagreed.

A car pulled around the corner. The electric door

to the garage began to rise slowly. It made a terrible racket.

'That's him, isn't it?' Johnny asked.

I looked at Johnny with alarm. I could understand him wanting confirmation if the light was playing tricks but under the circumstances there could be no doubt that the man in the car was Target B. Was Johnny losing his nerve?

'That's him,' I said in a calm, measured voice.

'You're sure?'

'Sure,' I said, every muscle in my body tightening to prevent me flying into a rage. I had to remind myself that he was the apprentice; I was meant to be the one with the experience. I needed to say something reassuring.

'Johnny,' I said, mimicking Bradley, 'I want you to talk to that man.'

'Talk to him?' he said, picking up immediately on what I was at. 'You want me to conduct an interview?'

'Find out what we want to know then choke him to death with one of these stinking socks I'm wearing.'

'Get 'em off, boss.'

We were both jumpy now. I wound down the nearside window. 'Are you ready?'

Our target wasn't much of a driver of large cars. He was being extra careful turning into the garage.

'Ready,' said Apprentice John.

'Remember the brief,' I said.

'I remember. I remember.'

'Make sure it's well wide.'

'Christ, but he's taking his time.'

'He doesn't know you're going to shoot at him.'

Apprentice John put a bullet in the chamber and took aim.

'Remember, you're a jealous husband who's a bad shot.'

'Fucking French farce,' said Johnny. His aim was steady, in spite of his jumpiness.

Johnny fired a single shot. The report coincided with the final clang of the garage door as it ground to a halt above the car.

'Bollocks,' exclaimed Johnny.

We waited a moment to see if there was any reaction. Any registration of the act would satisfy us, but our man hadn't heard the gunshot, and furthermore, the bullet hadn't made anything like a spectacular impact. In fact, neither of us was sure what it had struck. A pile of old newspapers at the back wall of the garage, perhaps.

'Christ.' The word was heaved from my stomach as I glanced up and down the street. 'Go again.'

Our man had come out of the garage interior and was opening the boot of the car.

'Hit something.'

Johnny hit something. He hit our man in the back of the thigh. It sent him spinning. Took him right off his feet. He bounced the back of his head off the pavement.

'Fuck SAKE, Johnny.' I dropped one foot on the accelerator and lifted the other off the clutch like a demented baboon and we took off down the street.

'I'm a jealous husband,' Apprentice John said. The tone he used to deliver this simple explanation suggested that though he had made a slight misjudgement, I was overreacting.

We didn't go back to the house. I kept driving.

'Where are you going?' Apprentice John wanted to know, coming across as innocent, almost cheery.

'I have to think.'

'Well, I'm thinking, too. Did you see his head bounce off the concrete?'

'Yes, I saw his head bounce,' I barked. 'Christ, Johnny . . .'

'So the little shit took a bullet. He'll live.'

I kept driving at a steady speed. I think I might have had Richmond in mind. It isn't clear in my head. As far as I could tell nobody had observed the incident, but I couldn't be sure. 'Christ, Johnny . . .'

I glanced across at him. He was smiling. He had those twinkling I'm-happy-because-I'm-making-trouble eyes. For some reason I was thinking about Captain Delaney of the New York Police Department on his way to his golf on Long Island. His contented disposition. His swerving around the drunk with a death wish. The tracks he and Captain Mitchell, Detective Sergeant Adler and Desk Sergeant Shields made in the morning dew as they swaggered up the fairway. Their playing around the corpse.

I decided I was thinking about Captain Delaney's adventure because it seemed more real than this new crisis my companion had visited upon us.

'We're safe,' Apprentice John assured me. 'Nobody saw us.'

Play around this one, he seemed to be saying. Get the ball in the hole. Move on.

He proceeded to tell me that, in his opinion, the mistake we had made was for the two of us to go there in the first instance.

'After all, Harry, an irate husband . . . he's going to jump in his car and go straight to his wife's lover by himself, isn't he? Not that it matters. Nobody saw us.'

I wanted to stop the car, smack his head and throw him out, but I didn't. I said nothing. I kept the speed steady. Kept glancing in the rear-view mirror.

'I take full responsibility,' Johnny said. 'I'll talk to Bradley, if you like.' He wanted to talk to Bradley directly. He was anxious to impress, even with his mistakes. His sort are always confident about their ability to explain away their outrageous behaviour and their mistakes.

The traffic moved smoothly. Everybody wanted to help. They didn't mind that Apprentice John had shot the little shit. Everybody was driving at a steady speed and I was watching out for wailing drunks in the road-way. I wasn't ready to take stock of our situation yet.

'We should ring him now, don't you think?' Apprentice John said. He didn't like my silence. He wasn't smiling any more. 'He should hear from us before he hears it from anybody else.'

Now, having blurted out the obvious, he felt foolish, and, for the first time since the shooting, he glanced behind us as he rooted in his coat pocket for the mobile phone.

'You can tell him about the head bouncing on the concrete,' I said finally.

It wasn't my intention, but that made him smile again.

A short time later, when I was swinging the car around Queen's Circle in Battersea, Johnny asked what I thought the chances were that Bradley and Clements would appreciate the circumstances and our good intentions and see that in all respects — bar his actually putting a bullet in the target's flesh — we had behaved in a thoroughly professional manner.

This was his attempt at mature reflection. He didn't even have the grace to wait a respectable length of time and pretend he had considered the consequences. I nearly crashed the car. I could scarcely bring myself to speak. The accidental shooting was so damaging, that for the moment I couldn't convey its seriousness. There was no mature reflection from me. I was in shock. I told him that there were two chances, and Slim had left town.

That didn't amuse him; nor, it seemed, did it bother him.

CHAPTER 15

I could feel my legs getting progressively shorter as I walked down the corridor to Bradley's office.

I knocked on his door and entered before I was invited. Obviously, he heard the knock but chose to ignore it, because I found him with a fork poised above an opened tin of tuna which he held in front of him at chest level. He greeted me with a lugubrious stare.

He was able to lift half a forkful of tuna from his tin and put it in his mouth without taking his eyes off me. There were no drops of oil, nothing dribbling down his chin, no fish flakes falling in his lap.

I was sure he had somebody else open the tin for him without his having to utter a word.

These little skills are disconcerting.

'Harry,' he said, as though there was some prospect of tuna fish coming my way, 'sit down.'

I sat.

'Harry,' he repeated, and I knew that he was going to take a long run at me, 'very few of us in life avoid being spurned, but you are one of the few.'

Ah yes, I thought, I'm in for it and here it comes, sooner than I had anticipated.

'I can see that,' he continued, 'and it interests me. It calls for an explanation.'

And there I sat, a fool radiant with hope. I remained

convinced that it was still possible for me to have what I wanted. Order in my life. A direction. Companionship. Love in a secret, parallel existence.

I was ready to rise above any obstacle, though the unrelenting expectation of contentment made me weary.

'But before we investigate just how much grease there is in your greasy little life,' Bradley went on, 'you can tell me about the shooting.'

'It wasn't a shooting, Jack . . .'

He put down his fork and his tin with remarkable speed and leaned forwards. 'Don't "Jack" me,' he said in a low, steely burr.

'It was an accident.'

'An accident . . .' His echo suggested it was fully appreciated that the distance between right and wrong could be short. He leaned back slowly in his chair. He still had me fixed with his stare. 'It was you, wasn't it? You fired the pistol.'

'No.'

'Thought you'd enjoy the kick.'

'No.'

'Thought you'd show young Johnny who was in charge.'

'No.'

'Just keeping your hand in. Is that it?'

'No.'

'You're a lousy shot, Harry. That's on record.'

'Johnny fired. He was unlucky. It was a ricochet.'

'He shot the man in the leg – and you let him.'

'I let him shoot, yes. That was the brief.'

'He's a worse shot than you and you let him at it.'

'Now you're confusing me, Jack,' I said. I wanted to protest – you teamed him up with me, I wanted to say, I didn't ask for him. You issued him with the gun. Furthermore, I'm patient, have a steady hand and will shoot when I'm sure.

I didn't protest. It wouldn't have done me any good. Bradley's judgement was never wholly based on the assertion of what was true or false; rather, it was the result of his weighing two propositions that either could or could not be reconciled.

Harry Fielding and Apprentice John were sent to do a job and had made a mess of it. Bradley was busy working through the consequences. He would concern himself with seizing whatever advantage might be had from the new circumstances we had created. That was how a seasoned opportunist would handle the inquisition that was to follow. Bradley would sit across from Clements and whatever panel of unofficial officials might be assembled, and with his usual forced freshness invite them to acknowledge his sharp appraisal of the facts and commend him on his pragmatism and common sense. They would then ask him to leave the room. There would be general agreement that Jack Bradley was not to be allowed to act at will on whatever opportunities might have arisen, but that the civil service class was very far from extinct as long as the Jack Bradleys were engaged.

'There's bloody hell to pay for this, and that's a fact.'

'I'm sure there is.'

'I'm your fucking mentor, Harry . . . Think about that.'

'I do. I do, Jack.'

'I put the lead in your pencil.'

'I know you did.'

'And this is what I get.'

'It's terrible. I know.'

'Clements wants to see you.'

'And Johnny, too, I expect.'

'Both of you.'

'Well, he would, wouldn't he . . . ?'

'Are you mocking me?'

'Christ, no, Jack.'

'I should have sent a pair of monkeys. Do you have any idea of what the consequences of this botched job might be?'

'I can only imagine.'

'Can you?'

His anger, I could see, was not entirely genuine. He had rested his fork on the lip of the tin and a small bead of vegetable oil was making its way down the spine. He stopped it with the tip of an index finger before it reached the worn leather-topped surface of his desk. He then rolled his finger on a piece of green blotting paper as though giving a print in a police station.

Never mind the man with the bullet in his leg, there was a great clutter of ink blots on his piece of blotting paper. Blotting paper must be hard to get these days, I was thinking.

'You're in deep trouble. You had better be thinking about another life.'

I noticed he had two flat thumbs. Good for prising open prawn shells.

'Are you listening to me?'

Another life? I might be found on the Serengeti plains sitting under a tree that looks like brains on a stick, unable to distinguish between being lazy and being a genius? No. 'I'm listening.'

'Clements is going to have your livers and I can't protect you.'

It was going to be all right. It was getting warmer outside. Life was returning to the vegetation. I imagined railway hedge-cutters were busy lopping their way through the countryside.

'You're not listening.'

The bag lady I had seen dragging her bundle about the streets on a kitchen chair the back legs of which were severely worn down, she would be glad of the change of season.

'I am,' I insisted. 'It was a ricochet. Just bad luck. We're sorry.'

Last summer I had seen a man score out on a beach the floor plan for a house he was going to build. I watched him move slowly from room to room, pulling on his chin, thinking it all out. Never mind some sleazy diplomat with a bullet in the leg. Had the bank lent the man on the beach the money he needed to build his house?

'You should have seen his head bounce off the pavement.'

Bradley kept staring at me. He was making a little nodding motion now. There was no debate. No thinking aloud. Bradley was not a debater, and nor was I. Suppress your personality, I had told Apprentice John – if you want to succeed in the firm don't express yourself. Accept the company you are in. Conceal what you learn.

'Bottom line, Jack, nobody saw us. We got away cleanly.'

I wasn't sure we had got away cleanly, but I wasn't about to dwell on that.

The nodding continued as he turned his head to gaze out the window.

'Brained himself, too, did he?'

'There was an awful thwack.'

He lifted the telephone and dialled an internal number and threw a switch to allow the conversation to be broadcast, through the speaker. 'Peter,' he said, 'you can have Harry Fielding now, if you like.'

'You have him there with you, do you?' Clements barked.

'Yes, and he'd very much like to have a word. Things simply aren't as they appear, he tells me.'

'Cocky as ever, I take it?'

'He wants a clap on the back and a cup of tea for his trouble.'

The black mud was back, filling my head more rapidly than before.

'Do you think he can find his way to my door?'

'Do you want me to ask? He's here, grinning at me.'

'We're on the boomer?'

'Yes.'

I could hear Clements wetting his lips.

'Harry Fielding,' he said, raising his voice slightly, 'step into my office.'

It was Bradley who was grinning, not me.

Before I had properly risen from the chair Bradley was dismissing me with a wave of his fork.

When I was passing through the hall the matron was coming down the staircase in slow motion. She was accompanying one of her charges who was descending in the electric chair-lift. She called to me.

'Mr Fielding, can I have a word?'

'Of course.'

I lingered while the chair crawled to docking position and the old woman rose unsteadily to her feet. She wouldn't let the matron assist. I smiled at the old woman and suddenly she was ready to talk. Talk at great length, I had no doubt, if I would just give her the start.

'All right, my darling,' said the matron. 'You go to the sitting room. Mr Fielding and I are going to have a chat.'

I didn't like the sound of that. *A chat* was worse than *a talk*.

The old woman moved away, uncertain of her direction, belatedly returning my silent greeting with a sudden smirk.

'Mr Fielding,' the matron said in a formal, confidential voice, 'your father has been drinking whiskey.'

I could see straight away that her tactic was to pretend there had been no previous conviction, and no discussion of the subject. I fell in with that.

'Ah yes,' I replied. 'He does that sort of thing.'

She led me away from the electric chair to a bench seat flanked by two narrow windows which gave a view left and right along the façade like archers' slits.

She dropped her voice further into confidential mode. 'It's the board's policy not to allow the consumption of alcohol in the house.'

I was being given the official line now rather than another discreet piece of friendly advice.

'You can't have them falling down,' I acknowledged.

'Indeed.'

'Taking a tumble down the stairs.'

'As you know, Mr Fielding, we have a lift and we have the chair, but with a drink or two . . . What I'm saying is that your father . . . Cecil has been drinking whiskey here in the home.'

'No.'

'I'm afraid so.'

'Has he been drunk?' Selective amnesia required conviction. There was an uncharacteristic earnestness in my voice.

'Well, no, but . . .'

'He's been making a show of himself, has he?' There was an old boy on a Zimmer frame by the flower-bed looking in at us through one of the slit windows. I felt the need to give him a little nod.

'No, but . . . he has been acquiring bottles of whiskey on a regular basis.'

The official finger had officially stiffened.

'Bottles?'

'Half-bottles, that is.'

'Where is he now?' The old boy by the flower-bed had not acknowledged my nod except to scrutinise us more closely.

Matron dropped her chin to indicate that there was a

modicum of indulgence if not understanding in her next remark. This I took to be part of the official protocol.

'You haven't been doing the needful, have you?' she asked. 'You haven't been supplying him?'

Having just sat down, I took this opportunity to stand up again. The half-bottle in my pocket wasn't sitting right. It was creating a conspicuous bulge. 'I bet he's been hiding them. There's probably more than the one on the go, if I know my father.'

This was slanderous, but I was on the spot. The old man approved of half-bottles, not half measures.

'He'd be good at hiding them,' I said. 'Have you searched the room?'

'Well, no. We don't search the rooms.'

I was surprised that I was getting away with this, but I continued. 'He's a bloody disgrace, so he is.'

I wondered if the singing would be mentioned.

'He hasn't been difficult, you understand.'

'Doesn't matter. He's lucky to be here. He has to abide by the rules.'

'A quiet word. That's all that's needed.'

'Half-bottles, you say. And where do these half-bottles come from?'

'We don't know.' Now, she was becoming more defensive.

'You leave it to me. I'll trim his wick.'

'Just a quiet word. No harm done, really.'

'Yes, but it isn't good enough, is it?'

'We don't want to deprive anyone of their little pleasures, but, what with the stairs . . .'

'There'll be others at it if he gets away with it. I know.'

'Indeed.'

Of course there were others at it. Of course they searched the rooms.

'And he's the very one to flaunt it.'

She was on her feet now and anxious to move on. 'Thank you, Mr Fielding. I'm glad you understand.'

'Oh, I understand, all right. Is there an off-licence near? Has he been going out by himself?'

'I don't think so.'

'Scuttered, was he? You can tell me.'

'That would be unfair. A little merry, perhaps.'

'He was scuttered. I'll search the room.'

Finally, she decided she should say no more. She thanked me and went about her work. There was no mention of Cecil singing in the lavatory.

'Here,' I said to the old man when I produced the half-bottle in his room, 'hide that in no man's land. Didn't I tell you, they're on to you.'

He was still putting on his tie. Still making a good knot and judging well the relative length of fat end to thin end. He was still tying his shoelaces and buttoning his flies. I was heartened.

He had taken to sitting with the smokers. So, we went there. The smoking room was occupied entirely by men. If he was desperate for companionship it didn't manifest itself in verbal exchanges, but there was some measure of mutual comfort.

'He's at it again,' he said, pointing to the window. The gardener was burning garden refuse. The bonfire was set against a blackened patch of wall across the lawn. The plume of blue smoke was filtering through the branches of a pair of mature beech trees.

'There's always plenty to burn,' said one of the smokers.

'What way is the wind blowing?' my father asked. 'Is it blowing this way?'

'There's no wind to speak of,' said another of the smokers.

'It'll be all over the bloody place,' said the first. 'You'll see.'

'What's he burning?'

'Garden rubbish,' I said.

Cecil said that he wanted to go for a walk, and so we set off round the grounds. He didn't waste much time pretending that he wanted to stroll. He led me directly to the gardener with his bonfire as soon as we had left the building. He was determined to establish precisely what it was that was being burned.

'How are you?' I asked Cecil as we approached.

'Fine. Couldn't be better. They treat me very well. Staff couldn't be better. Food is good. I'm getting my sleep. I'm getting exercise. I have books.' He ran all this together. It made me feel bad.

He greeted the gardener with a sharp hello and scrutinised the material in the teeth of the flames. 'That's a good blaze you've got there,' he said. His tone suggested that a pertinent question was to follow, but none was forthcoming. The gardener acknowledged my father's words and continued with his business.

'How are you?' Cecil asked me without taking his eyes off the fire. 'Are you well? You shouldn't come here every day. It's not necessary.'

I didn't visit every day, but I nodded. 'I like talking with you, Cecil.'

Whether or not he believed the words they seemed to bring him instant release from some torturous riddle. He no longer needed to know what was being burned. We moved on.

We made our way along the shaded path on a long curve that took us to a neglected alcove in the bushes. There was a broken bench which was still serviceable. Before the old man sat down something in the flower-bed caught his eye and he turned a bit of earth with his foot.

So, he had been burying the empties after all. He had chosen his spot well. It was secluded. You couldn't get a clear view of the overgrown alcove from any of the windows.

We sat together in a grand silence, and presently a few others from the home joined us.

Cecil had assembled a little group, of sorts, but he didn't trust them. 'They pretend to be asleep,' he told me later. 'They pretend to be your friend, but they'd live in your ear if you let them.'

I knew not to judge these words too harshly. I knew the old man was just trying to keep a clear perspective.

'Of course, they know they're not fooling anybody. That's the thing about this place.'

He shared his whiskey with one of them only, a healthy old fellow whose mild manner, one suspected, was an effective cover for a mischievousness that bordered on the criminal. He was the only one of the sorry group to whom I was introduced. He and Cecil sat slightly apart from the others.

'This is Bill.'

'Hello, Bill.'

'Hello, son,' came the reply in a Liverpool accent. He shook my hand and gave a broad smile to reveal a set of shiny yellow teeth. Even Liverpool Bill of the firm handshake didn't get to see where the bottles came from or where the empties were buried. Didn't know that they were right under his nose.

'I fancy a swim,' said Bill, out of the blue.

'Do you?' I replied.

'I'm getting him in,' Cecil said.

At first I didn't understand. The old man saw the confusion on my face and explained impatiently.

'Into the baths.'

'Ah yes. Of course.'

'Getting him a steam and a rub-down.'

'I fancy a swim, though,' Bill persisted. 'I really do.'

Cecil ignored the specific request. 'I wouldn't mind a rub-down myself,' he said.

I was going to offer to make arrangements, but the old man stopped me with a raised finger. He didn't want to give details in front of the others.

There was another old fellow who, for whatever reason, was not going to get to the soap baths on Cecil's ticket. Nor was Cecil about to satisfy the curiosity of the women in the group. With them he was going to keep any report of his life vague and pass himself off as mysterious.

Bill turned to me and said, as though for the first time, 'I really would like a swim, son. In the sea.'

Clearly, it was important to him that a fair-minded stranger knew of this need.

'I have the togs,' he said. 'They're up in the room.'

The fact that Cecil heard this aside didn't seem to matter. It didn't make him revise his plans for a rub-down.

'Swimming in the sea,' said one of the satellite women. Her white, nylon hair was swept back in a style that facilitated her openly earwigging across the narrow divide. 'The shock will kill you.'

Cecil and Bill both ignored her, but she didn't mind. She was content to have made her contribution. Her contentment, however, didn't prevent her from attempting to broaden the subject.

'You'd need a stiff drink, at any rate.'

Cecil opened the bag of sweets I had brought him with a jerk and stuck it out in front of her. He wanted to stop her in her tracks. She smiled, put her hand in and pulled out seven or eight wrapped sweets. Cecil made no complaint. He chose to ignore her scoop.

She swapped the sweets from one hand to the other, then lined them up on the bench in some secret order known only to her, with the same indulgent smile on her face.

'No, no,' Cecil said fiercely when the third fell into rank by the second. 'If you're not going to eat any put them in your handbag.'

She ignored him.

'Your bag, for God's sake. In your bag.'

Why wouldn't she accept his gift? She didn't get it at all.

Bill shook his head sorrily and Cecil responded with a sclerotic nod.

CHAPTER 16

Apprentice John came back to the house with a rip in his tongue. I found him looking at it in the mirror. It wasn't a big rip, but it must have been sore.

'How did you get that?'

'I just got it, all right?' he said, baulking at my impertinence.

The tongue was swelling and it made him sound like a simpleton.

'Yes, but how?' I persisted.

'I caught it on an ear-ring.'

'An ear-ring.' Now there was a picture.

'Yeah. I had my tongue in her ear, and I caught it.' He didn't say whose ear.

'Looks sore.'

'I don't want it going septic.' He was still inspecting it. Still marvelling at the damage.

'No. Of course you don't. Cheap ear-ring, was it?'

The mouth closed. He glowered at me.

'You should put something on it.'

'You think so?' he said resentfully.

He was going to show me the ripped tongue again but I stopped him with a hand gesture.

He went and got his *Animated Nature*. He came into the kitchen to enlighten me further.

'Listen to this – about the Dodo . . .' he said with his thick tongue.

I was willing to listen but knew I should sit down.

'The Dodo. Ah yes. Go ahead.'

'Sit down,' he said, without looking up from the page.

'I'm sitting.'

'"Its body is massive, almost round, and covered with grey feathers; it is just barely supported upon two short thick legs like pillars, while its head and neck rise from it in a manner truly grotesque . . ." He's talking in the present tense. There were still dodos on the planet . . .'

'I'm sure I saw one of them recently . . .'

'"The neck, thick and pursy, is joined to the head, which consists of two great chaps, the one far behind the eyes, which are large, black, and prominent: so that the animal when it gapes seems to be all mouth."'

'Yes – I've seen one of those at the firm. Seen it waiting outside Clements's office. Probably the only proof of Clements's idea of undercover work.'

Apprentice John was not to be distracted or deterred. I rested my chin in my hands.

'"The bill therefore is of an extraordinary length, not flat and broad, but thick, and of a bluish-white, sharp at the end, and each chap crooked in opposite directions. They resemble two pointed spoons that are laid together by the backs. From all of this results a stupid and voracious physiognomy . . ."'

He had hoisted himself up on to the kitchen worktop. He was settling in for a long lecture.

'It says here that besides its disgusting figure, it has a

bad taste, but it's easily taken and three or four of them is enough to feed a hundred men.'

'Clements likes the exotic.' I said. 'He'd like one of them on staff. If it didn't work out, he'd eat the evidence, feathers and all.' Then, I changed the subject. I pointed to his mouth. 'You never know with a thing like that,' I said. 'Shouldn't take any chances.'

He didn't know whether or not to take me seriously.

'No . . . really.'

His ripped tongue was getting at him. He gave a shape to a curse using his stomach muscles, and went off to the bathroom. A moment later he let out another stomach-propelled curse.

'What?'

There's nothing here I can use.'

Target B's embassy officials had conducted their own assessment of the shooting at the garage. The bullet in Target B's leg, they decided, had been intended for their colleague's head. Target A, the real prize, had enemies in his own backyard. Naturally, the firm was keen to encourage any split among the brethren, but very reluctant indeed to be compromised again directly as they had been in New York. This was stressed in an odd meeting I had with Clements. He personally summoned me to his office late one evening at short notice. Just me. No Bradley. No Apprentice John. No little helpers.

He peeled his glasses off to the left and held them out, seemingly for the benefit of some short-sighted invisible demon gnome who was in his employ and squatting on his desk waiting to do his master's bidding. The momentary break in his gaze served to emphasise that he could read a man's character just as easily without his close-work glasses.

Tactically, it made sense to look away. For a time I concentrated on the invisible gnome. I thought Clements might take exception and say 'This behaviour hurts England. Thank you and good night.'

He didn't. He knew I was paying full attention.

Having been given virtually nothing of the bigger picture on the job to date, I had expected a dressing-down over the shooting. Instead, I was treated to a lecture on moral responsibility, which, I suppose was always going to be jumbled into the day-to-day affairs of that building.

When I got back to the house Johnny was pacing the floor. He had just had a call. He wanted me to go with him to his parents' house in Blackheath because the place had been burgled.

Naturally, he was concerned and wanted to reassure his mother and father, but really, he was going because he had been summoned.

'Are you coming?' he asked.

'No,' I replied.

'You're too busy?'

'No. I'm just not going.'

'Look, if they need us in this place they'll call on the mobile. Bradley said there would be notice.'

'I know. That doesn't bother me.'

'Come on, then. With you along I can get out quicker. Besides, you'll like them.'

'Call a policeman. Get a social worker. I'm sure they've given the glazier or the locksmith their tea already.'

'You're a hard bastard, Harry.'

'I don't like visiting people's families.'

He accepted this as some kind of legitimate explanation, and that surprised me. My surprise must have shown because he persisted.

He told me his parents would treat me as a king-maker. His mother would fawn over me and his father would slap me on my back and fill me with his single malt whiskey. They would, of course, ignore their own son, he warned. Such would be their relief at his having got himself a position with some responsibility, a life with structure. A job that required discipline and had prospects.

'We won't stay for dinner. I'll buy us a curry on the way back.'

'I said no.'

'Right. Suit yourself.' He went hunting for the car keys. He put his hand in the pocket of my jacket which was draped over the back of the couch, and fished them out.

When bitterness masks humanity it is usually a near-perfect eclipse. Not in Johnny's case.

In the car on the way to Blackheath I conducted an interrogation. I was curious about his family background.

'Did you ever tell them about your aid work? That must have made them proud.'

'I might have told them. I don't tell them much about my life.'

'You didn't tell them about beating up the volunteers . . . just that you were doing charity work.'

'I don't give them details.'

'So what did you tell them about your new situation?'

'I told them I was working for the firm.'

'And that you couldn't give them details . . .'

'Something like that.'

'You want me to tell them you're doing well?'

'Could you, please?'

'Tell them that really, you're the other half of the toolbox.'

'That would be nice.'

We had been drinking and we were amusing ourselves, but there was something in Johnny's manner that betrayed a great unease, and that was another surprise.

'I remember telling my old man about working for the firm . . .' I said.

'You told him about a job?'

'Now, if I did, do you think I'd tell you?'

'Hey, I'm not looking for details. Just yes or no. Sometimes you have to let something out. Something like the truth – right? That isn't a question, by the way.'

But it was a question, and a good one, at that.

I made no reply. I was thinking that, apart from his exotic inclination to wait on people, Apprentice John had no manners. I would have to talk to him on the matter, because being without manners meant that he didn't fully listen and if he didn't fully listen he wouldn't fully comprehend, and one day that might prove costly.

'Are we in a hurry?' I asked. 'Are we late?'

'No.'

He was moving from one buttock to the other in the driving seat. He was like a prancing vulture waiting to get in on a kill.

'Then slow down.'

It was a lovely calm evening. There was a full moon and a mackerel sky. I wanted to enjoy being back in London. I wanted to glide through the streets and not give a damn.

As we lurched rather than glided with the traffic, I rehearsed a little mantra about my good fortune —

I had been taken into the fold. I had a regular salary. There was the prospect of substantial responsibility, promotion, comradeship, a pension plan, club fees paid. But something about Clements's attitude bothered me. I thought again about my recent after-hours meeting with him. I realised that his lecture on moral responsibility had come from another place beyond his usual brief; some deeper, more personal well of worry. In retrospect I was sure he had questions he had decided not to ask that night. Now that had me worried.

Stop, I told myself. Enough. Concentrate on enjoying the rush of balmy London air.

My heart was sinking. I couldn't bring myself to believe any of my good fortune was coming to me straight. I knew better.

Better than Apprentice John.

I wasn't really in from the cold, nor was my troubled friend.

Apprentice John got out from behind a column of slow-moving buses, taxis and private cars and took off up the other side of the road. I was pressed snugly into my seat.

And by the way, I demanded of myself – which clubs are these that figure in this new existence?

Apprentice John pulled across just in time to avoid collision with an oncoming truck carrying tulips from Holland.

'What does he think he's doing?' Johnny wanted to know. 'Nearly killed us, the bastard.'

He wasn't going to slow down, nor was he going to cease taking chances. He was looking to pull out again.

I spread my toes in my shoes, rested my head on the seat back and gazed up through the sunroof at the moonlit mackerel sky.

'This burglar . . . what did he get?' I asked.

'Nothing.'

'Nothing?'

'The old man confronted him. He came into the bedroom . . . like you've seen on *Crimewatch*.'

'Was there violence?'

'Some. Pushing. The old man was knocked to the ground.'

Johnny's fawning and convivial whiskey-drinking scenario lost all credibility. These people would be very shaken. Why hadn't he told me this earlier?

When we got to the house Johnny's old man was still smarting with rage, and he was a little drunk from the brandies he had been given by his wife to calm him.

He wasn't at all what I had expected.

He was tall and fat and had decided he wasn't meant to be both. You could see it in the way he moved, the way he tried to redistribute his bulk. He wouldn't sit down and he wouldn't shut up, and he managed to ignore his wife completely. He had developed a false personality and that seemed to come out of the body thing. There was a lot of talk about nothing and all of it was related to him. He was afraid of a lull in the conversation. Doubtless, had he felt a lull coming on he would have broken into a whistle. Crises or no crises, he needed a signal from you to the effect that you didn't mind him being a tall, fat bastard before he properly engaged.

Anyway, I didn't like him, so I didn't send a signal. I felt sorry for Johnny's mother, sorry for their trouble, but I took my ears off and put them in my pocket. Johnny's old man was too busy blathering to notice.

We got our whiskey. Johnny's mother saw to that. She was incapable of ignoring anybody. We also got biscuits on a saucer.

'He had a go at the burglar,' she reported anxiously. 'He went downstairs when we heard the noise. I told him he should call the police.'

'You rang the police, dear,' he retorted. 'I had a go. I'll try anything once,' he said glibly. It was a hot kind of glibness.

His wife managed to reply forcefully but without a direct reproach. 'You can be sure that the person who first proposed that came to a sorry end.'

Johnny and I looked to each other and he let out a sharp guffaw. His mother was quite flushed herself from the brandy. Her hand moved involuntarily to her face, raised it seemed on an invisible string, to brush aside a stray lock of hair. Her own hand took her by surprise.

Apprentice John didn't say much. He just asked after his younger sister, Marsha. Where was she, he wanted to know. She had been living in the basement since she had broken up with her boyfriend. The boyfriend, Johnny told me, was a soldier, and he had been hanging around the house ever since the split.

'Well, I chased him, anyway,' Johnny's old man blustered. He took another mouthful from his glass and looked expectantly at the brandy bottle on the magnificent sideboard. 'He got the message quick enough.'

'Thank God Marsha is away,' his wife said. She had said it a dozen times, no doubt. It was now a little prayer of thanks.

'Bloody quick he was, out that bloody door.'

He caught his wife's eye and indicated the brandy bottle with a curt nod.

Now why did I think the big man had no qualms about lumbering down the stairs to intrude upon his daughter's privacy any time it suited him?

When I got out of bed early the following morning I found Johnny sitting on the bare stairs, brooding.

The swelling had reduced a little but it was giving him trouble. He was still in pain when he talked. He was doing a good job of pretending it didn't bother him and there was something vaguely ridiculous about that.

'How's the tongue?'

'It's fine.'

'Let me look.' I pushed past him and turned.

'Don't bother.'

'No. Let me see.'

He opened his mouth slowly, as if revealing his molars to God's dentist.

The colour wasn't right.

'Septic.'

'Septic?' The alarm showed immediately in his eyes. 'How could it be septic? It's in my mouth.'

'Exactly. In *your* mouth, Johnny.'

'Are you laughing at me?'

'All right. It isn't septic.'

Another stomach curse. This one fully articulated, and acknowledging the medical fact. But he was determined to talk out his denial.

'I have these dreams, right . . . ?' he said.

'Oh yes . . . ?' The scepticism was immediately apparent in my voice.

'They're all about meeting people . . . famous people . . . bad people.'

The last phrase had a childlike innocence to it. What horrendous stories had he in store for me?

'Such as?'

'Well, Mussolini, for one.'

'You dreamed you met Mussolini?'

'I had a talk with him.'

'About what?'

'About engineering.'

'What – ball-bearings and such?'

'No. I'm serious. I met him by chance on Tower Bridge. He was admiring the engineering of the bridge.'

'And he spoke to you in English?'

'No. He spoke Italian and I spoke English, but we understood each other.'

'You're getting him mixed up with Hitler. Hitler visited London. He liked Tower Bridge.'

'Look, if I say it was Mussolini, it was Mussolini.'

'So, you and Mussolini talked about Tower Bridge?'

'Yes. He seemed to know a lot about building bridges.'

'And nothing happened? You just stood there talking?'

'Now, here's the strange thing – you see, I knew he was a bad bit of work so, while we talked, I gradually moved over to the rail and took him with me. He was impressed with my knowledge of the history of the bridge.'

'Was he, now?'

'I leaned right back over the rail and pointed up at the towers. He leaned back and I thought – right, this is your chance . . .'

'And?'

'He leaned right out above the river . . .'

'And?'

'I couldn't get him to go over the rail. I reached down, took a hold of his legs but I just couldn't tip him over the rail. His feet were stuck to the ground.'

'And?'

'And he just laughed. He laughed, that is, until his hat fell off and went in the river, and then he got angry.'

'And you dived in after the hat?'

'No. I changed tactics. I invited him back to my flat for coffee. You see, I had left my knife in my other jacket on the back of the door.'

'Johnny, there's something wrong with you.'

'For some reason, he got even more angry when I

mentioned coffee in my flat. He must have thought I wanted to get up on him, the bollocks. I was hardly going to tell him about the knife, was I?'

'No. I could see why you wouldn't do that.'

'Anyway, I woke up before I could gut him.'

'These dreams you have, I bet they're all like that. I don't want to hear any more about your meetings with famous bad people.'

'Interesting, though, isn't it?'

'Read more books, Johnny. That's my advice. Let other people make up the stories. You'll enjoy it more.'

I should have recognised that he genuinely wanted to share his sense of wonder at these bad operas his subconscious was sending up the dumb waiter. He wanted intelligent discussion on the matter, not patronage.

'They come around again and again,' he said, choosing to ignore my comments. 'Each one of these people has their own smell.'

'Really?' I said, and pushed past him and made my way to the kitchen, where I found there was nothing to eat. Apprentice John had, in spite of his sore tongue, eaten everything.

He went out late that night and came back in the small hours. He was drunk and in an agitated state. He had a rock in his hand. He gripped it tightly. There was blood on it.

I found him scavenging in the kitchen, eating out of the packages I had bought in the corner shop. When I came in he had one hand in a box of cornflakes. He was cramming the dry cereal into his mouth. The bloody rock was weighing something beyond its mass in the other hand.

I knew better than to ask directly where he had been and what he had done.

'Sit down, Johnny.'

'I don't want to sit down.'

'Sit down.'

We are half animal, but it was time for reason and reflection.

He abruptly sat down on the table with his back to me. He took the cereal box with him.

'Do you want milk on them?'

'We have no milk,' he mumbled.

'There's other things to eat.'

'You want me to get milk?' he asked fractiously. 'I can get milk.'

'No,' I replied. 'I'm not hungry.'

He held on to that rock tightly, but the hand lay lifeless on the table beside him. I moved around the table so that I wasn't talking to his back.

'You want me to make a sandwich?'

'No. No sandwich.'

'You had some trouble?' I said, nodding at the rock. It was dark and dense. Limestone.

'The people you meet in the middle of the night . . .'

He was trying to be funny, but he wasn't carrying it off. He was too wound.

'Which ones are these, Johnny?' An idea was quickly forming in my head. I had an ugly picture of his sister's ex-partner, the stalker, lying somewhere with his head caved in.

CHAPTER 17

I had been out watching my ex-wife with Bradley. They had gone to a restaurant. When I got back to the house I was in a sweat, and, I decided, altogether too gracious.

I found Johnny sprawled on the couch in a drunken sleep, spittle dribbling down his chin. We had agreed there would only be moderate drinking. I smacked him on the head.

'Get up, ya thick get.'

I knew I was still sounding too gracious for him to recognise me as anyone other than a stranger, so I gave him another smack as he surfaced.

'It's your pal Harry.'

I knew there would be a slight delay between me identifying myself and his recognition, so I was able to anticipate the first swing of his right fist.

'Harry . . .' he shouted, as he rolled with his own punch and somehow managed to turn the momentum into the force that got him rapidly, if unsteadily, to his feet. 'Harry . . . it's you,' he said stupidly, and wiped the spittle from his chin. 'What time is it?'

'Where were you?'

'I was right here,' he said with conviction. I could see his brain hadn't yet kicked in.

'Right here,' I repeated.

'Waiting for you. And here you are. And, by the way, don't hit me.' Behind this lame rebuke he was trying to blast a way through the alcohol haze to some memory of any task he might have forgotten.

He hopped around the floor trying to get a shoe on a foot that he wasn't entirely sure was his own.

'What you have to realise is that this waiting around is as frustrating for me as it is for you,' he said with a floppy confidence.

He got the shoe on. Discovered there was another shoe for another foot.

'I'm backing you up and now it's come to this – it's down to words . . .' He still couldn't remember what it was he had neglected. 'It's down to you calling me names and shit.'

While he had the other foot in the air I smacked his head again and he toppled over on to the couch.

'Getting up,' I said, 'that's a tough one. Often the hardest thing in the day.'

The haze was beginning to clear. Johnny realised it would be easier to put on the second shoe if he remained sitting on the couch. He shook his head and made a point of relaxing for a moment. He did some kind of exercise with his jaw and rubbed his damaged tongue on the roof of his mouth. I could see him changing tack and moving into confessional mode.

'You know what bothers me about being drunk?' he said. 'I never know who it is that opened the door in the small hours and let in the horse that shat in my mouth.'

It didn't come as a surprise that I had no answer.

'What are you hitting me for, anyway?' he suddenly wanted to know.

'I'm stepping in to remind you about drinking.'

'Intervention . . .' Apprentice John said. He was using Bradley-talk.

'You like the sound of that, eh?'

'Well, it's action, isn't it?'

'I thought you'd like it.'

'I'm for intervention,' he declared decisively, a short time later. Bradley had certainly been indoctrinating him. The new term seemed to fit perfectly an approach that until now had gone without a satisfactory label in Johnny's life. 'Aren't you for intervention?'

'If I was, I wouldn't tell you, would I?'

It was a rhetorical question, but he answered with a degree of humility.

'No. You wouldn't.'

The antibiotics the doctor prescribed for Johnny finally kicked in. Nothing more was said about the ripped tongue. Nothing was ever said about the woman with the cheap ear-rings and, presumably, septic ear lobes.

Time heaped up against our faces. I was sure I could shave away an entire day with a few slack strokes of my razor.

Johnny went back to Volume One for a 'Summary Account of the Mechanical Properties of Air'; chapters also on Puberty, Sleep and Hunger. He had gone on to study the Crocodile and its affinities, Multivalve Shell Fish, and was now reading about Lythophytes and Sponges.

The contracts were about to be exchanged on the house in Muswell Hill at last. I had to do the final clearance. I bribed the dustbin men to come and take away a pile of stuff that I couldn't dump on my disgruntled and rather sad brother.

The gang boss shimmied over to me when I beckoned from the front door. He spoke to me in a surprisingly thin voice.

'Do you want something out?' he asked, before I had even opened my mouth.

'Yes. I do.'

'We don't do washing machines or fridges.'

'No white goods.'

'We don't do cookers.'

'There's no cooker. It's small stuff, mostly.'

'They all say that. Give me a look, then.'

He whistled to the driver and made a quick, complicated signal. It's difficult to be quick and subtle in the same instant, but this man could do it with his hand signals.

'This way, captain,' I said.

He fell in beside me. The truck drew up alongside us and kept abreast. The rubbish harvest speeded up on both sides of the street. Even the pasty-faced one with the ginger dreadlocks and headphones changed gear effortlessly to make time for the unauthorised collection.

The captain worked his tongue around his teeth as I pointed out the material that was to go. When I had finished he nodded and said: 'Seventy.'

I didn't agree immediately. Not because I didn't think it was a fair price – there was a lot to go out. It was just I realised that once this stuff had gone I would be turning the key in the door for the last time.

'Seventy – between the lads,' he felt he should add. He was anxious to move on.

'Right. Seventy.'

He went to the door and called them in with a hooked thumb. They came through the house like a pirate raiding party. The job was done quickly. Nothing more was said. I don't know how much I gave the captain. Eighty quid, I think.

Then there was just me with the key in my hand.

The old man wanted to go to the church I assumed he occasionally attended. He wanted to pray for my mother. He wanted to act his age, to get beyond his grunting and to bare his pain.

I worried about returning to the neighbourhood with him. I was afraid he would insist on visiting the house that was no longer his and that he would break down.

But we went anyway. Something was working itself out.

For my old man every journey was sacred, and the dignity that required was reassuring. On a journey like this you might have heard a little angel singing on the dashboard.

Coming up Crouch Hill, however, he began to get agitated. It had been going smoothly up to that point. I had been driving at a moderate speed and the traffic was flowing easily.

As I turned into The Broadway and made for Park Road and on to Muswell Hill he attempted to loosen his tie, but only made the knot smaller. He wound down the window.

'We have a little time to spare,' I said. 'Why don't we stop? Take a walk in the park.'

In fact, we had quite a bit of time to spare. Because I was anxious I had turned up early at the home. I had got him into the car and out through the gates with all the dispatch of a rescue mission.

'Are you sure we have time?' he asked. His chest had tightened along with his tie knot. His breathing had become shallow.

'I'm sure. Do you want to go to Alexandra or Queen's?'

Alexandra Park or Queen's Wood? I could see him struggling to decide. He was momentarily stuck.

'We could go to the lake,' I said. 'We'll go to the lake. I'd like the lake.'

'Yes. That would be the thing to do.'

I shouldn't have given him an option, I was thinking. I should have suggested Queen's instead. It was further from the house; the one less frequented. He had used Alexandra Park for his meetings with his cronies.

'I'd like that,' he added unconvincingly.

I found I was driving faster now we'd committed ourselves to the one instead of the other.

I got a parking space not far from the lake. They were ripping up the road but had finished for the day. I moved a few traffic cones and reversed into a space that was meant to be kept free. When I saw the old man looking out at the roadworks I realised that he might be confused by the lines of cones, the trench and the displaced earth, but he sprang the lock as soon as I had switched off the engine.

I thought he wouldn't be able to get out of the car

without assistance, but he was determined. He held on to the open car door, stood his full height and yawned. It was a big yawn. It ground the stiffness out of his jaw.

'Come on, then,' he said, as though it were just me who wanted to go to the park. He led the way. The roadworks caused no difficulty.

He started off slowly. You can be patient and nervous at the same time. Slow work makes me nervous.

'You're busy at your desk, then?' he asked. *At your desk*, I understood, was a euphemism for just about any activity associated with my job with the firm.

'I am.'

'Doing what?'

This wasn't a real question, or rather, a real answer was not expected. It was an expression of approval.

'There's a lot of waiting.'

'Ah yes.'

He was on the lookout for a familiar face on the paths and benches, and so was I. Anyone he might connect with. Anyone who might provide a distraction.

'You've checked the post for me?'

'Yes,' I lied. 'Nothing at the minute.'

'Any envelope with a window – just write deceased on it and put it back in the post.'

I said that I would.

That made him feel better. He gathered speed. He liked the wind in his face. He seemed to sense the clouds rolling up from the horizon and over our heads.

'Any calls for me?'

What calls might these be, I wondered? Did he think I was camping in his house?

'No calls at the minute.'

'You *are* checking?'

'Yes. I am. Regularly.' I made a mental note to ensure he got his post and to make some effort to see to it that his friends had a telephone number for him at the home.

'But you're busy . . . I know that. Nothing new to report, then?' He was now referring to my personal life.

I wanted to tell him that I had recently discovered that I liked to read when I was drunk; that I found it reassuring.

'No. Nothing, really.'

'Analysis, is it?' he asked, casually returning to the subject of my new job.

'What?'

'Intelligence analyst? That's it, isn't it? Putting the jigsaw together with a mallet.'

'Something like that.'

This was another show of general approval laced with a healthy scepticism. It was also him trying hard to take his mind off his rediscovered grief. I was desperate for a familiar face. A neighbour or one of his cronies to pass the time with him before evensong.

It was a perfect evening in the park. Everything was synchronised and the spaces between every human being perfectly judged. It gave me a bad feeling. Cecil, however, gained strength enough to practise being grumpy.

'Christ on a bike. Is there anybody looking after this place?'

The park was looking particularly well, and he knew

it, but what better to practise on than something in which he could find no real fault?

'This way,' he barked. He pushed me in the direction of the lake.

I sat him down on a seat by the lake and told him again bluntly that the family house had been sold. He pretended that he was aware of this and, once again, shame and fear registered in his eyes.

I responded by looking at my watch.

'You've arranged for my post to be diverted?' he asked, in his best civil service voice.

I assured him that I had.

'Well, that's all right, then.'

I wanted to tell him about my new family, Clements and Bradley. I wanted to tell him about Bradley and my ex-wife. But I was bigger than that. I was looking out for him, wasn't I?

We were handed hymn-books when we entered the church. The service had already begun. There weren't many parishioners attending so we had our choice of pews. I moved towards a pew at the rear, but Cecil marched on up the aisle to the front. As gracefully as I could, I altered course and followed. Both clergyman and verger acknowledged Cecil's arrival with their own discreet signals.

Mrs Harvey was there in a beaded beret and tweed coat. When she caught sight of Cecil her face lit up. She gave a restrained but excited wave. Cecil saluted her formally.

The congregation were standing, singing a hymn. Cecil made his way through the pew to the outer end where he sat, then knelt for a moment. I could see he was catching up, and soon he was standing with a hymn-book open at the current hymn, opening and closing his mouth, making noises of the familiar words, as the tone-deaf do.

After the service Cecil remained seated. Mrs Harvey came over, flushed with good-neighbourly favour which Cecil was happy to return, albeit self-consciously. He kissed her on the cheek, something I am sure he had never done before. He was to come to tea, she said, no special arrangement needed. He was distracted but he gladly accepted her invitation.

When she moved off down the aisle he leaned forwards, his eyes staring, his hands clasped. The verger approached and with a discreet acknowledgement, as before, drew the old man's attention. He seemed to be able to distinguish between prayer and reflection.

'Cecil,' he said, 'we've missed you.'

'Derek,' said the old man, 'look at this.' He pointed to the shoulder of the pew in front of us. 'Wood-worm.'

The three of us leaned in to examine the little clusters of oak dust and the holes that went with them.

'Oh, bugger,' said the verger. 'That's new.'

'Derek, this is my son, Harold.'

'Hello, Harold,' he said, giving me the smile an air hostess gives when asking whether you want chicken or beef. 'You're welcome.' A robust defender of the faith, he was already looking around for the clergyman, who was seeing the last of the congregation out of the church.

The reverend promptly responded to his verger's

beckoning. He came to us and heartily shook Cecil's hand and mine, and was shown the woodworm holes.

'Bugger, bugger, bugger,' Derek muttered, as the reverend bent down and got as close as he could to examine the holes.

'You won't see them,' the verger advised, 'just in case you think you will.' He addressed his remark to me but it was for the reverend's benefit. He was afraid the reverend might let the side down with some overgenerous comment about one of God's smaller creatures. The verger turned to Cecil. 'I thought we were rid of them.'

The reverend issued a sudden blast of air from his mouth, which scattered the dust. The verger disapproved, but stopped short of open criticism.

'What do you think, Cecil?'

'You'll have to act fast.'

The reverend came out of his crouch with a red face and broad smile. 'We will, won't we.' He extended his hand in my direction and I shook it. 'Harold,' he said firmly.

'Reverend,' I replied, with equal firmness.

He couldn't resist another squint into the network of holes. He screwed up his eyes and peered inside as though woodworm might in the end bring about the demise of the Anglican Church. It wasn't entirely a fierce scrutiny of the enemy. His squint carried some measure of wonder.

He came out of his crouch a second time. 'I don't suppose you're interested in ringing our bell, Harold?' he said, the redness in his face replenished, the same broad smile struck.

Tea was provided in the rectory in Cecil's honour after I had made a poor joke of getting in an electrician to electrify the bell-ringing.

I didn't know that the old man had been Keeper of the Belfry. He had never told me. I marvelled at his secret dedication. His continued silence on the matter fascinated me and produced its own silence. The visit to the church had both frustrated and reassured him.

When we got back into the car I knew that he wanted me to drive past the house. He wanted to make sure his wife was not in the front room with a TV dinner on her lap or sitting on the bottom step of the staircase in the hall, talking to her sister on the telephone.

I could see him summoning all his resolve to resist asking me to make the short detour that would take us down the street. I could see him tightening up again. I could see all the benefit of the church visit draining away.

'Do you want to look in at the house?' My mouth was running ahead of my thoughts.

'If you like,' he said with difficulty. 'If there's time.'

'Of course there's time.'

The house was in darkness except for the hall. I stopped the car and Cecil wound down the window. The estate agent's sign was still lashed to the railings.

'The hall light is on a timer,' I said, and he looked at me curiously.

'For the burglars,' he said from a great distance.

'Yes.'

We sat there in the car for ten minutes or more. He stretched the worn Expandex strap of his watch. He worked it off his wrist. He repeatedly cleaned the face of the watch with his thumb. Slow, forceful strokes. All of this he did without being conscious of it.

I tried to think of something grown-up to say. Something outside myself.

Nothing came.

He drew slow, deep breaths. I could do nothing to assist in his fight. I could only bear witness.

Finally, he turned to me to acknowledge that fact.

'Time to go, son.'

Before I took him back to the home we stopped to have a drink in a pub. I thought he might want a short to steady his nerve. Neither of us had been in this place before. It was full of men in coats standing at the bar and Cecil warmed to that immediately.

We pushed our way through and got our drinks. Cecil wanted to stay at the bar.

'You don't have to visit me every other day,' he repeated. 'I don't expect it. I don't need it.'

'I like coming to see you.'

He scoffed. But it wasn't a dismissive scoffing.

'Get that down your neck,' I said, pointing to the contents of his glass.

'I will.' He drank.

'I was thinking of getting another dog,' he said, and maybe he was, but he was also finding another way to demonstrate to me that his memory had not deserted him. 'I know I said I wouldn't, but, I've been thinking . . . When I get out . . .'

We were three hours late getting back to the home. The duty nurse was concerned and made a point of mollycoddling the old man, which, he let her know, he didn't like at all.

CHAPTER 18

This new existence, these new priorities – which if I
am honest were very much like the old priorities but
with more urgency – seemed to be working out. It
seemed to be the right measure of good deed and
dirt for Harry Fielding. Aunt Kate had visited Cecil.
She had gone to the home and had flirted with the
old man by opening up her handbag and having a
conversation with it. This, of course, drove him mad
with contradictory emotions.

My brother and his wife had belatedly taken up some
of the running with the old man. The affair between
Bradley and my ex-wife had shown me what I chose to
see as strength rather than toughness. I was impressed
with my own patience. I was taking some of my own
advice – I had cautioned Apprentice John to always
look a second time, whoever the target might be; to
watch for longer than he felt necessary; to see what
melted away.

That was something I had learned a long time ago
from my father, and he had learned that hunting for
stolen treasures after the war. Aside from his work for
the Trading With the Enemy Department at the Public
Record Office, he liked and understood embezzlers and
crooks. He wallowed in other people's dirty business
and had acquired a very particular kind of patience

from which I now benefited. Applying this patience ensured a consistent belief that a person could act on their desires.

But other people often have a different sense of order and act accordingly.

I drove to the house in Muswell Hill. The *For Sale* sign was still up by the gate but it now had a *Sold* banner across it. I looked in the window. It was bare inside. The new owners had not yet moved in. There was no sign of Cecil.

I went next door to Mrs Harvey's. I thought the old man might have gone in there; thought I might find him in a daze, drinking tea at her kitchen table.

Mrs Harvey had not seen him and was more than ever concerned that I was neglecting him and that wherever he was he was being mistreated.

'You haven't seen him,' I repeated. I tried to get the balance right between a weighty concern and casual acceptance. I tapped my chin with a knuckle. Suggesting that I was perpetually worried about my father would be no defence against her suspicion. In her estimation, not knowing where he was every instant of the day was simply unforgivable.

I wrote the number of my mobile phone on a scrap of paper and gave it to her. 'You'll ring me if he shows up, Mrs Harvey?'

She nodded, then seemed to soften a little.

'It must be difficult . . .' she said. 'Won't you come in a minute, Harold?'

'Thank you, but I won't, Mrs Harvey,' I said. There was a chime in her name this second time and she liked that. 'I think I know where he might be,' I lied.

'That's good news,' she said. She was easily taken in and appeared to be genuinely relieved.

I got in my car and drove away, but was unsure of where I should go next. I decided to park a little way down the street and look in some local haunts.

I went to the pub where he used to sit with some of his cronies, talk knowledgeably about the wars of Africa and exchange prescribed drugs.

There was no sign of him. The barman knew who I was asking for but said that he had not seen Cecil for some time; then, belatedly, he asked how the old man was faring.

I went to the park near by. He went here for his medical exchange programme, too, but also to pound out a couple of circuits when he was grumpy.

No sign.

I got back into the car and drove to the soap baths, another of the haunts where he and his cronies congregated. It was a long journey across the city for an old man but he went twice a week and insisted on travelling by bus and tube instead of taxi, which he could have afforded.

I knew many of his friends by sight and had talked to them, but I had no addresses. They were all like tramps to me. Cecil liked the company of scruff, good-time Charlies and misfits, many of whom were charmed by him and were consequently more loyal than one might have expected.

When I stepped on to the terrazzo floor and smelled the soapy air that was tinged with bleach, I felt sure he would be there.

None of the attendants had seen my father for a long

time, but I did meet Reggie, one of his shaky old pals. He had been in to visit Cecil in the nursing home, he told me, and he had talked to him on the telephone.

'They listen in, you know,' he informed me, 'not that we give a damn. We're way ahead of them.'

'He was telling you he was coming out, was he?' I ventured.

'Yes. He was just building up his strength.'

'When was this, Reggie?'

'Last week. Wednesday . . . yes. I took a taxi to see him.'

'And what did he say? Did he tell you his plan?'

'He didn't tell me any plan. Just that he'd be getting out.' Reggie was getting annoyed. He didn't want to give anything away, but he was concerned for his friend. 'I told him he should take a taxi and he said he might do that.'

I had called Reggie out of the steam room. Now, scratching his pot-belly, he turned uncertainly on his great, flat feet.

'Have you talked to Rita?' he asked. 'She might know where he is.'

Rita was the mysterious woman whom the old man had announced would be moving in with him one day. That was as late as last year. He had not introduced her or described her to me. He would only tell me that I would like her. He was putting in a house alarm for her sake. Well, the house alarm was installed, but Rita never came.

Reggie recited Rita's surname, said that she lived in Shepherd's Bush and could be found in the telephone directory.

'She has something to do with the Hemlock Society,' he added with deep scepticism. His hard frown was instructing me that my father would be even more sceptical than he, and that there was not the remotest possibility that Cecil would be thinking about putting poisonous drops in his ear.

I wrote down Rita's surname and thanked him.

'When you find him you tell him Reggie thinks it's a fucking liberty he's out and hasn't come to see me. Lovely to see you, boy,' he said over his shoulder as he slapped his way back towards his bench and was swallowed by the steam. 'You're a good son.'

I got Rita's telephone number. I rang, but there was no answer. I drove to the address listed in the directory. There was no answer at the door. I had a quick look through the living-room window. From what I could see of the interior it was cluttered with antique furniture, books and biscuit tins full of papers, photographs and buttons. I sat in the car for some time, watching and waiting. It was a small terrace house. The bushes and shrubs in the small front garden seemed to be planted for privacy. I could imagine the old man bringing his hedge clippers wrapped in brown paper to do a job on the more vigorous growth.

It was late in the afternoon when I again found myself in Muswell Hill. I stood outside the house for a moment looking at the alarm, and at the jumble of weeds and overgrown shrubs. It was still warm and there was a breeze. The mouth of the laneway that led to the gardens at the back beckoned, so I went.

The blistered wooden door in the back garden wall was ajar and swinging gently on its hinges. I don't know what prompted me, but, as I pushed open the door, I called the old man's name as though I were entering his bathroom.

A strong gust of wind came in behind me, all of it channelled through the garden doorway, and blasted the overgrown vegetation in all directions.

I found him lying in the long grass.

His eyes were open. He was on his back gazing up at an uncertain sky. He had wound a twist of grass around one hand. I put my ear to his chest, then, to be sure, I put two fingers to his neck to feel for the non-existent pulse. Then I sat down beside him. I seemed to know what I should do and how I should feel.

I knew I could talk. I talked to dead friends when I was alone driving the car. Why not to my old man when he's lying in his own back garden.

'I'd better just do this,' I said aloud, and rang for an ambulance.

I turned at the waist, stretched over him, passed my face back and forth across his field of view. I tried to catch him out. I listened for his slow laugh and his heavy breathing. I acknowledged the perfect pitch of an ancient memory – my father playing dead on the beach.

I settled back as I was.

How long had he been lying there? Had he collapsed but remained conscious while I was in the soap baths? Had he been conscious while I was peering in the window at the front of the house? Had he wound that clump of grass and held on in expectation of someone coming to his aid?

I didn't ask him these questions.

'I thought I might find you here,' I said.

You can lie to the dead as well as to the living. They are none the wiser.

I didn't want to close his eyes yet. Nor did I want to engage his stare. I was sitting with him, after all.

I drew my knees up, rested my forearms on them and looked out across the neighbourhood. It wasn't a question of having been slighted by his silence, by his deadness. I needed to take in the minute geography. To establish with certainty that it was here, in this familiar place, that he had fallen.

A smell of wood stain came and went with the blustering wind. Somebody was painting their garden shed, protecting it against the elements.

'Your pal Reggie, he says it's a fucking liberty that you're out of the home and haven't contacted him.'

There was no one at any window. Nobody watching. To my ears the sounds of traffic were exceptionally clear but softened, and that kept me alert because I knew it couldn't be right.

'I have to ring Johnny,' I said. 'You haven't met Apprentice John. He works with me. He'll need to know where I am.'

Just because he was dead that didn't mean he would now, suddenly, know my friends and associates.

'I keep this phone off most of the time. Took your advice.'

I rang Johnny. He said he would come over immediately.

Then I told the old man about this mysterious job we were waiting on, and of my deep misgivings.

'It isn't sitting right,' I told Cecil.

I was surprised at the measure of concern in my voice. It wasn't the lack of information that bothered me – the tight lip usually protected the man in the field, as well as the operation generally. It was something about Clements and Bradley's attitude. Now here I had to be doubly careful, for my own feelings with regard to Bradley's affair with my ex-wife had to be suppressed if my thinking was not to be clouded.

I didn't tell Cecil about Bradley and my ex-wife. I let him think she and I were getting along famously.

Now I was talking to the old man without moving my lips. I wasn't trying to catch him out. Nor was I looking for his approval, though I was doing what I think he would have done. I was salvaging rather than pleading. I was being pragmatic. That forced some clear thinking.

I wasn't asking him to hover over Clements and Bradley's desks or to read their thoughts, but rather to pass to me a bitter wiliness and an appetite for conspiracy and corruption which outstripped my own – and I had first-hand experience of both. I would gladly take with it all his knowledge of the wars of Africa from the dawn of time if that was an integral part.

'I know too many dead people,' I said, reaching out and touching his hand. You can tell me that now. The underside of the car is bouncing off the road under the weight of corpses.

There would be no more mumbling from the old man. Christ, he'd be talking to me now as never before.

Not giving a damn for my good intentions.

Not caring about anybody else.

Lumbering around after me, camping on my door-step, talking to me but never telling me what he wanted.

My eyes fixed on a jar of shrivelled holly berries in the window of the rotting garden shed. I had never rung my friend at the airport to get the strips of carpet to insulate it. Instead, Apprentice John and I had used the shed to pile up broken furniture and rubbish – whatever was left behind after the binmen had taken the extra load. It was all still there for the new owners to clear out. I had missed the jar of berries the old man had collected for the birds in winter. I would have taken the jar had I noticed it. How had I missed a jar of red berries?

Apprentice John came on the scene quietly. He was crouching beside me before I was fully aware of his presence.

'Well now, Johnny,' I said, 'we have a situation here.'

'All right,' he replied with a soft earnestness.

I thought he might make a move to feel for the old man's pulse, but he didn't. Nor did he put a hand on my shoulder, nor offer immediate condolences. He looked from one of us to the other with a concerned expression that was rigid.

'This is my old man.'

Johnny nodded. He must have thought I expected something more, because then he squeezed Cecil's forearm lightly in acknowledgement and rose to his feet and went into discreet waiter mode.

'You've called the ambulance?' he asked.

'I have.'

'I'll go round the front. Keep watch.'

'No. It's all right. Stay.'

'Stay? Of course I'll stay.'

He withdrew several paces and stood in the shade of the wall. He swung about sharply when Mrs Harvey's face appeared above the six-foot wall. She had brought out a kitchen chair to stand on, and even though the legs of the chair sank into the soft clay of her herbaceous border, she seemed ridiculously tall.

'Cecil,' she called out in a small voice. She had finally seen me and my father in the grass from her back-bedroom window and had hurried downstairs. 'Oh dear God, Harold . . .'

'We've called the ambulance,' Apprentice John told her. 'It's on its way. Perhaps you could keep a lookout for it.' He gave her a quick, nervous smile and with an outstretched palm indicated that she should go immediately to her hall door.

'Yes. Yes, I will.' She quickly climbed down from her chair and hurried up the garden. 'I'll ring Simon, Harold,' she called out before she entered her kitchen, 'he'll come straight away.'

Simon was her doctor son. He lived thirty miles away.

'Go through the house,' I told Johnny. 'We'll let them in through the front door.'

I didn't want the old man taken out past the uncollected bags of garden rubbish and have the ambulance men stepping in dog shit.

'Keys?'

'No.'

Apprentice John was already moving towards the back door and reaching into his pocket for a pick.

It didn't take him long to gain entry.

'That's Apprentice John,' I told the old man. 'He likes to think he's the other half of the toolbox. Bit of a rogue, as you can see . . .'

Once he had thrown the lock Apprentice John entered the kitchen with all the confidence of a head waiter.

'Bit of a thug. But we like him, don't we?'

CHAPTER 19

An action – that was the term used. We were taking an action. Not in the legal sense. Quite the other thing.

Bradley had summoned me to brief me further on the job and to offer his condolences.

'Look,' he said, 'I know this is a bad time for you, but things are happening and we must be ready.'

Mr Clements wasn't well and had taken leave of absence for a short time, he informed me. Clements was, of course, directing affairs from his retreat.

Bradley sat in Clements's Bodleian chair and talked into his sandwich. What was it with these people eating on their laps instead of going to the canteen or out to a restaurant? Were they setting a good example to facilitate cutbacks? Was it a crackpot directive to do with some new puritanical drive?

Bradley wasn't bright enough in the nutrition department to know any better. He seemed only vaguely disappointed that most of his sandwich filling was mayonnaise, but he allowed that disappointment to dictate the tone of our conversation.

Perhaps this picnicking was some kind of new theory about interrogation methods being put into practice.

He opened one half of his diagonally sliced mayonnaise sandwich to investigate further, but I knew he would never find the source of his disappointment.

There was a smear of sauce in one corner of his mouth that changed dimensions when he spoke into the sandwich.

He didn't fill the broad seat of the chair any better than his boss. His correct posture and his deliberate, quiet voice suggested that he was for rational thought, tolerance and regeneration. But he just couldn't get through the mess between the two slices of bread. I wanted to reach across Clements's desk and smack him on the side of the head.

'The poor chap you put in the hospital,' he said. 'We have a proposition for him. His son is coming to visit. We're going to take him off the plane and put him in our hotel in Pimlico for a short time, and we're going to see if dad has a location for his brother-in-law. You follow?'

'I follow,' I said, but I was a little slow putting the picture together, perhaps because I had begun to think of our 'hotel in Pimlico' as nothing more than a billet for a misfit and his apprentice.

Bradley pointed out that Target B's son had the same enemies as his uncle, Target A. He liked using the generic titles. It allowed him to be patronising in a sophisticated clubhouse manner. 'I think you know how important it is that we find Target A as soon as possible,' he said.

'I do,' I replied. And I did, but I couldn't quite see Johnny and me bringing the kidnap victim his dinner.

'Mr Clements is keen to stress that this is an exceptional action to counter an exceptional threat,' Bradley informed me.

I detected a note of bitterness in his delivery, but the clubhouse manner quickly resurfaced.

'Again,' he said, making direct eye contact, 'sorry about your dear old dad.'

This expression of regret was also to signal that the briefing was over. I thanked him and turned to leave.

'Oh, by the way . . .' He opened a drawer, took out two automatic pistols and placed them on the desk. 'You'll need these. Don't go bloody shooting each other.'

I picked them up and weighed them in my hands.

'Well?' he barked impatiently.

I told him they would be conspicuous if I put them in the pockets of my suit. They would have been all right in the pockets of a coat, but I hadn't brought my coat. I asked if he could lend me a bag.

Reluctantly, he gave me a nice leather zip-around satchel.

'I'll want that back,' he said.

The parish newsletter was published the day before my father's funeral. It contained, in the form of an additional slip, an obituary for Cecil Fielding, Keeper of the Belfry. It marked his passing, stating simply that he had been a bell-ringer for over twenty years until ill health prevented him performing the task. It commended him on a duty faithfully discharged.

He had left no specific instructions for his funeral. It was entirely consistent with his having been a dutiful and neglected civil servant. I assumed that had he done so he would have asked for a modest, conservative send-off. But what about his subversive streak? This thought prompted me to look at the pew where Bradley and the sickly Clements sat, just behind my ex-wife. Perhaps Cecil would want to surprise his former masters by revelling in the limelight, I decided. I imagined him being buried on *Songs of Praise*, with the television cameras craning up over his coffin to take in the choir in full throat, leading the congregation in a rendition of 'Joy to the World'. The congregation was made up of friends, the Muswell Hill neighbours and a party of hand-picked scruff all smelling of soap. I was chief mourner and Aunt Kate was beside me in the front pew.

She was so impressed, and that was as Cecil would have wanted it.

I heard my out-of-key singing, my stumbling over the words in the hymn-book. Could I tell the vicar in the church in Muswell Hill that the standard funeral service wasn't enough? Could I get them to play a recording of 'Sailing By', followed by the shipping forecast while they put him in the ground?

Perhaps I could get Kate to make one of her Quaker speeches. Something simple and dignified. She would finish with something scurrilous and then she would weep because it would go unchallenged.

Dead men's talk is never about their own funerals. They leave you in the lurch.

Reggie was sitting with Rita, the old man's erstwhile companion. She looked well in her glamorous, moth-eaten clothes. They were staring out into the long distance. I could see a deep reserve of humanity in her blemished face, and a pervasive confusion that was part of her being.

'Look at that,' Reggie said.

'What?' she asked.

'The dirt.'

He was referring to the smog on the horizon, I think.

'I've seen it,' Rita said. She was upset, of course. Her relationship with Cecil, so far as I knew, had been well grounded, if somewhat sporadic.

'Big one there,' Reggie said a short time later, pointing to a distant jet crossing the sky.

'What?' she said. She squinted into the light.

'The plane. Coming out of Heathrow,' he added, chancing his arm.

'I see it.'

There was another pause. His eyes lowered again to the horizon, and then he must have fixed on a group of small figures in the middle distance.

'All the children.'

'Yes,' Rita said. She opened a packet of cigarettes, took one, lit it. Instead of offering Reggie a cigarette directly, she held out the packet and said, 'I'm putting these back in my bag.'

'Go ahead,' he said without rancour.

So she did.

'You'd think they'd do something about it, wouldn't you?' she said with a jerk of her chin forward into the landscape.

'The dirt?' Reggie asked without much interest.

'The dirt,' she confirmed.

They fell silent, perhaps because of all that they knew about existence. I was tired. I wanted to lie down in long grass in another place. At the firm's expense I would feel the dampness seep through my tailored suit. I would not speculate whether or not the fat cargo plane flying slowly across the sky was crammed with push packs containing one-day rations for people in desperate need; nor would I wonder if the stretch of Underground track passing under the small of my back had been equipped with a sensor designed to detect a biological attack in the piston effect of the tunnel.

I would gaze up into the sky knowing that I would learn nothing, that I could let my mind rest. A column of carpenter ants marching over my body would go unnoticed. I would be oblivious to bullet rain. I would only know that I had slept because I had woken.

The reductive analysis was off-key, but on that day it was better than getting drunk.

I looked again at my father's friend Reggie. Somebody would be updating my file, I thought. Father deceased.

Erwin, another of my father's cronies, came to speak to me. He signalled to Reggie that he should introduce him. I had seen Erwin at the steam baths with Reggie but had not met him. After Reggie had introduced us Erwin took me aside.

'Harold,' he said, leading me away by the arm, 'I want you to know if there is ever anything I can do for you, you must ask.' He spoke with a German accent that had a knuckly East End London inflection. Certainly one of the old man's crew of scruffs. He wanted to play godfather, so I let him.

'You don't know this,' he said, 'but your father saved my life, and I don't forget.'

'I'm glad to hear it, Erwin.'

'You see – you don't know. Before war broke out I came from Munich to London and they interned me at Ascot. They put me sleeping in the stables. They gave us bromide to make us tired and to reduce our libido. I escape the Nazis and they want me not to have sex with myself. You don't understand? No? Good. Neither do I.'

'You met my father during the war?'

'He befriended me. It wasn't so easy as you might think to befriend a refugee Jew. They wanted to deport me but Cecil prevented it. Class A Alien they were saying. Dangerous. But he said no. He got them to reduce it to Class B. A risk. They kept me two and a half years, then they let me out. I'm still a risk, Harold, I'm happy to say.'

He gave a sudden, hearty laugh.

'Cecil would appreciate that,' I said.

'He would. And I miss him more than bloody Reggie, or Rita. Now, I'm going to help you with your dad's stuff. I'm going to pack his clothes and get him sorted.'

'It's all right, Erwin, that's all been taken care of.'

'You've done it, have you?'

'Yes.'

He seemed disappointed. He wanted to help, but there was nothing practical he could do, and because there was nothing he could do he got angry. 'You moved him out quick enough.'

'I packed all his things,' I told him again.

'No. I'm talking about moving Cecil out of his house.'

'No choice, really . . .'

237

'He never wanted to go to a home.'

'Well, he did choose to go.' I was feeling bad again, but that was my business.

'Bloody home wasn't the place for him. He should have come and lived with me. I would have looked after him.'

'We didn't know that was an option.'

I saw the anger drain from his face as quickly as it had risen. 'Well . . . he wouldn't have put up with me. Too proud, you see.'

'We both know that, then, don't we?'

'We do.' He gave another sudden laugh, this one shorter than the last. 'You want a lift? I can take you anywhere in my car.'

Really, at his age and with his foul temper, he shouldn't have been driving.

'No thanks, Erwin.'

'Just like your father. We'll see you at the baths, maybe?'

That was when Clements's messenger approached.

CHAPTER 20

The mobile phone rang. I didn't recognise the voice. The decoy name came first. If the voice on the other end says yes to the decoy name, assuming it to be an operational cover, then they have shown themselves immediately to be an interloper. Rudimentary, but surprisingly effective.

'Graham?'

'No.'

'Harry?'

'Yes.'

I was told to wait in the bar of the Randolph Hotel.

'How long do I have to wait?'

'Don't know.'

'Will I be collected?'

'Don't know.'

'If I'm not there you can reach me on the phone.'

I didn't like the cockiness in the voice. I didn't like his clipped patronage. He must have been one of the security mob, one of the Georges, trying to sound like he had a seat at the high table.

'You just wait in the bar. You do as you're told.'

The line went dead. I stood for a moment and let the Oxford traffic swirl around me. Then I went to the Randolph, sat down at the bar and got slightly drunk.

It was very quiet. I got bored very quickly. It doesn't usually work that way when I get slightly drunk.

I stared out the window across at the Ashmolean Museum. My wife had once told me that it housed Guy Fawkes's lantern. 'You'd be interested in that,' she had said when things were still working between us. Could I nip across the road to look at one exhibit? And, of course, there had been a daring art theft. On New Year's Eve they had broken in through the roof.

I had the excuse I was looking for to defy the order to wait in the bar. Call it a professional interest coupled with an appetite for art. In my life as an understrapper I had done my share of house – and office – breaking for the firm. I could nip across the road for a brief case study. And, I could take in the lantern.

I slid off the stool and crossed the street to the museum. I'm happy to read when I'm drunk. Newspapers, novels, biographies. Anything to hand. I don't take any of it in, but it's always a lush glide that leaves me with a vague sense of wonder. This, I decided, would have the same effect.

I felt virtuous and well behaved entering a grand building on a sunny afternoon. My feet made a satisfying sound. Medieval ivory carvings. Hunting scenes. Drawings by Raphael and Michelangelo. I would just do a quick tour, I decided. Bombard my eyes. I seemed to take corners with one leg stuck out straight like a Dutch skater.

Did I see somebody rest both arms on an ornate chest of drawers and put their head down as a tired child does?

I kept looking up at the skylights, alert to any

weakness in the defences. There would have been improvements since the robbery, of course.

I talked to one of the attendants. She pointed me in the direction of the room that had housed the stolen work. She gave me a thorough, matter-of-fact account of the raid, without pointing out where exactly the thieves had gained entry.

'Is this where they came through?' I asked another attendant in another room.

He wouldn't say, but confirmed that they had gained access through the roof.

That was the spot. I was sure. I quickly lost interest in the robbery.

The gallery was full of pink and yellow flesh, cows and other Dutch skaters. It felt good. I wanted to stay, but the mobile phone rang.

'Michael.'

'No.'

'Harry?'

'Yes.'

'Where are you?'

'The Flemish School.'

'Where?'

'The Ashmolean Museum.'

'You were told to wait in the Randolph.'

'I'm in the wrong neck of the woods altogether. I'm actually looking for Guy Fawkes's lantern.'

There was an icy silence, but I kept it cheery just to annoy him. 'Are you waiting for me there?'

'No.'

'Am I being collected by car? I'm coming down the stairs. I'll be across the street in a minute.'

'Wait outside the museum.'

'If you like.'

'You never learn, do you, Harry?'

The connection went dead. I took my time descending the staircase in the museum. Being told by a supercilious stranger that you never learn is an irksome affair. I know such things get said by small people to make you think they know more than they do, and consequently should be ignored, but it can give you the hump.

When I came out into the sun and stood by the entrance I observed a man about to cross the street from the hotel. He was dressed for the outdoors and for a colder day. As I watched him step into the road between the traffic the cigarette in his mouth presented itself as having been put there by someone else. He had got used to it; he had no choice but to inhale and exhale through it, forcing a quick burn rate and an excess of flying ash.

He came over to me without ever looking at me directly.

'Harry,' I said, a pre-emptive introduction. Before he said anything I knew he could talk with the cigarette in his mouth.

'Yes. I know.' He was a cool one, in spite of the ash. I decided that when he wasn't smoking or talking with a cigarette in his mouth he was eating with his mouth open, and still managing to be cool. Furthermore, his general manner led me to believe he changed his socks once a week.

'Was I just talking to you?' I asked him. You can't always tell.

'No.'

You see.

'You got tired of waiting in the foyer?' he asked me.

'In the bar.'

'In the bar . . .' He cut across my path. 'No. This way.' He was already walking towards St Giles.

'Nice day, isn't it?' I was going to insist it was a nice day.

'Lovely.'

Definitely one of the Georges.

'I was in looking at the art.'

'Were you?'

'Lovely.'

'You should have been at the hotel. That's what I was told.'

'I know. I never learn, do I? Are we late?'

There was no reply. George was being conspicuously professional and I was carrying myself particularly well for a man who was slightly drunk.

We crossed St Giles. At St John's College he pressed the night bell and a small door opened in the wall.

'Good afternoon, gentlemen,' the doorkeeper said. 'Straight through, please.'

I was led through one square to another, more secluded. Then we passed under a black statue of Charles I in his ornate armour, through a small archway and into the expansive garden beyond. A network of ancient sprinklers in the rockery and flower-beds was hissing and gurgling intermittently.

The doorkeeper stopped here without explanation and stood to observe my bad-tempered companion lead the way to another door in another wall. He opened this with a small magnetic button which he had on a key-ring.

'The gooseberry garden,' grumpy George announced over his shoulder.

Now why did he do that, I wondered? I could only assume it was a piece of information he had been instructed to give me.

'There's no gooseberries,' he added humourlessly.

We passed through another door in a soft stone garden wall, and this took us via a passage to the lawns of Trinity College, where there was a wedding reception in progress complete with a fancy tent for serving afternoon tea, and a quartet. It was a lavish affair with perfectly poised guests stepping over the stripes in the lawn. The sun got brighter and the people more beautiful as we approached, and I didn't like that.

I hadn't been told about a wedding. It was Clements's daughter who was getting married. There was no denying the family genes. They wouldn't pass for mother and daughter if he was wearing a dress, but she had the same shape to her face, and the spring-loaded jaw.

George led me to one side and put me standing by the marquee. 'There won't be time for tea,' he mumbled, and went off to report to Clements who, I observed, was in a half-time huddle in what might have been a lawn cricket match between the Royal United Services Institute and the Parliamentary Intelligence Security Committee. I was hoping they wouldn't look across at me. I didn't want to know those people.

George managed to unscrew the cigarette and make

it vanish. Was it my imagination, or did that action make it difficult for him to speak? When he spoke to Clements, Clements gave a discreet acknowledgement without looking my way. He issued another brief instruction. George signalled to me that I could, after all, get myself a cup of tea. Evidently, there would be a delay while Clements finished the story he was telling. His kind know not to cut short their socialising with influential people, because the stories and the small talk are all the firm's business.

I stood with my tea, which was in a china cup, and I watched Clements's daughter. I caught her eye once, briefly, when she glanced in my direction.. I raised my cup from its saucer to toast her and gave her a big smile, which she returned. Whoever might be watching me, I was showing myself to be a good civil servant, and my father's son. It was a reflex rather than a calculated strategy. I was showing I understood that often we in the firm preferred to remain ignorant of the matter in hand, and that kind of ignorance is always cheerful.

I thought about my ex-wife. The first time I had observed her on my return to London. I had watched her through the living-room window of the house we had once shared, having resolved to make an attempt to win her back.

I observed her telling a story and it was a lovely thing to watch and I was certain in that moment there could be a second chance for us. I didn't want to intrude, so I waited in my car. The feeling I got from watching her animated figure was so good that I felt compelled to look away, indifferent to my fortune, and count the lamb-chop trees that arched over the road. Then I saw it was Jack Bradley she was entertaining.

She had stood beside him at the graveside and sent me a private signal of compassion.

I was still being cheerful when I felt grumpy George clutch my elbow.

'We're going now,' he said, taking the cup and saucer from my hand and putting it down on the linen-covered trestle table. He tried to give a sinister edge to his words but the tone was too conspicuous to be menacing. He was clumsy as well as grumpy. He kept too close in his escorting. He was another poor judge of human movement. He propelled me along ever more swiftly.

'What's the hurry?' I wanted to know. 'Is there a fire in the pet shop?'

No answer, of course.

I was presented to Clements on the other side of the door leading to the gooseberry garden. Even in the gooseberry garden, George was bunched up behind me.

'Harry,' Clements said, shaking my hand. He looked pale but otherwise healthy. His handshake didn't feel right. It wasn't induction day, and I wasn't senior enough. Wasn't anywhere near the inner circle. Trouble.

'This way,' he said.

I could feel George putting a guiding hand on my arm so I made a point of not moving off on cue. His grip tightened with impressive force. I jerked my arm free. Clements paused and looked at me questioningly.

'Mr Clements,' I said, 'can we let the air out of him and fold him away?'

Clements glanced from me to the now angry and grumpy George. Away from the wedding party he didn't look overdressed in spite of his formal attire. 'You can mind me, Harry.'

He gave a barely perceptible twitch of his head. There was a slight delay before George did as he was instructed. I thought he might produce his lighted cigarette from a fire-proof pocket, but he withdrew in a professional manner; that is to say, he returned to the door in the garden wall without giving me the hiding he was sure I deserved.

Clements and I stood where we were for a moment before he spoke again. He looked about our private gooseberryless garden. I saw him change his mind. He walked on, giving another barely perceptible jerk of his head to which I was to respond in an equally professional manner.

We went through several doorways and passages and out into the street. He set a pace that was brisk, even military. I could feel the adrenaline in me trying to rise above the alcohol. I kept level with him. I wanted to say: whatever it is, count me in.

We crossed several junctions, then, in a quiet street, he stopped in the doorway of a dwelling. He drew a key from his pocket and we entered. I was struck immediately by the heavy, not unpleasant musty smell of ancient fabric and oak floorboards dried by an ageing central heating system.

'Nice house,' I said.

I didn't think it was his. And it was too special by half to be a safe house, even for special clients. It belonged to a friend, perhaps.

I was thinking about how he had worked the key in the lock. He wasn't used to it. He didn't know he had to pull the door towards him to make sure the mechanism turned smoothly.

It was a splendid seventeenth-century interior. He told me there were shells in the attic and between the ceiling and floorboards immediately above us, for soundproofing and insulation. He couldn't imagine that I might just know such a thing about seventeenth-century houses.

There was a stained-glass window on the first landing of the narrow, what seemed to be three-quarter-scale staircase. The glass featured panels with darkened exteriors of the Holy Land interspersed with bursts of Divine light. In the fret beneath it read: WHAT OF THE NIGHT? THE WATCHMAN SAID, THE MORNING COMETH, AND ALSO THE NIGHT.

Clements saw me taking in the piece.

'Magnificent, isn't it?'

'Yes. It is.'

More tea. I was worried by the tea and the handshaking and this trip to the friend's house.

Then he spoke to me through his forehead. It's fortunate, he said, that all my monkeys do not recognise the wisdom of these biblical words.

He told me to wait in the drawing room. He virtually ordered me to sit in one particular chair. He didn't want me snooping. Once an understrapper, always an understrapper – a fair assumption on his part.

He went to the kitchen and prepared the tea.

I looked in the ancient bookcases. There were rare volumes of essays on political history, theology and art. No inscriptions in any that I picked up. No ex-libris panel.

Below, behind delicate brass lattice cabinet doors, there were books on astronomy, and an extensive collection of opera records. In one recess beside the chimney-breast in the far wall there were several icons from the early Russian Orthodox Church. In the matching recess, a medieval crucifix.

For a man who could be conspicuous and clumsy when it suited, he was very light on his feet. He suddenly appeared in the doorway bearing a laden mahogany tray.

'Milk or a slice of lemon?' he asked in a quiet, rich voice that suggested he was already enjoying my company.

'Milk, please.'

I watched him pour. It's funny how you think you can tell a man is intelligent, thoughtful and ruthless from his small, everyday actions. I got the impression he would think about the distance a fish had travelled across the ocean bed to his plate.

He served from a nineteenth-century tea service which had NOT MADE BY SLAVES printed on the china sugar bowl. He put spoons on our saucers and milk in first.

'A Chocolate Oliver, Harry?' he asked, holding out the thin, china plate.

'No, thank you.'

He pretended that I had failed to meet his expectations. I pretended to enjoy his little game.

'Absolutely my favourite.'

In spite of his intelligence, his thoughtfulness and his

ruthlessness, there was something unconvincing about him; like a politician with a lisp. But then, maybe that was just more of his act.

'Mine, too. Fancy that.'

He had slipped away from my father's funeral before the graveside service had finished. He again offered his condolences and then got down to business. 'Jack Bradley has you busy, does he? You and, ehh . . .'

'John Weeks.'

'You and Johnny.'

'We listen a lot to *Woman's Hour*.'

He wet his lips. 'You stay in at night, both of you?'

'African music on the World Service. And Johnny is learning to read.'

'You're keeping a close eye on him? Reporting to Jack?'

'Yes.'

There was something odd about being honest about being sneaky.

'Good,' he said with an impressive vagueness. 'Good,' he repeated, from a greater distance still. He took an eccentric route to the window. He looked out at nothing in particular. He wanted me to be aware of his cultivating his haziness.

He turned suddenly from the window with the same fixed grimace he had presented before. If I do this with my face, he seemed to be saying, and you try to match that with the vagueness in my voice, you will only get confused; I will then break your concentration with a sudden dropping of my spring-loaded jaw.

'Jack tells me he's more of a liability than an asset. You'd agree?'

The words came out of his mouth in a fierce matter-of-fact tone. If my shiftlessness bothered him on his daughter's wedding day he didn't let it show.

I was sure he was aware I had been drinking, but he chose to ignore it, and I could only assume there was a purpose.

'He's learning,' I replied.

'He's a dangerous young man. That's what you're saying.'

'You want that, don't you, Mr Clements? Under control, of course.'

He made his way back to his chair and sat down heavily. He drank a mouthful of tea. He waited until I did the same before continuing.

'He's reckless. Right?'

I was surprised by my own recklessness; my uppitiness. The static charge that went with it must have been hopping off me.

'He's nervous, but only because he wants to do the job thoroughly. He'll get over his nerves.'

What job was this I was speaking of? My nerves were jangling. In spite of the alcohol, I was wound tight.

'A real hothead, Bradley says. And, evidently, a bad shot. Bit of a bloody cowboy, I'd say.'

'Yes, sir. At the moment.'

'I can see him on his musical horse – you know those horses, Harry, don't you? The ones in the old westerns that gallop along furiously to the soundtrack.'

'I do, sir.'

'That's our man, Johnny Weeks.'

'Bang, bang, sir.'

If up to this point he had been unaware that I'd been drinking, it was obvious now.

'Johnny is a ruthless and immoral adventurer.'

Was this a judgement or an insight shared? I had learned that they are never quite the same thing. It was all being put so that I would agree with his comments.

'Yes, sir. That puts it very well.'

'Useful in the field, of course, if there's a brain at work, and there is loyalty.'

There was no doubt in my mind that Clements was troubled. He needed to test the components of my convictions against his own. He wanted me to see him as a man forcing himself to go against his true nature, doing it discreetly, but with an iron will.

It was a pretence, or it was as it seemed. I couldn't decide. I wanted to say: stop right there. Tell me I'm drunk.

'As I say . . . Johnny is a little nervous at the moment.'

'You like him, though. You think he's good. Good for the Service.'

'Yes,' I heard myself say. 'I do.'

'Jack chose you and Johnny for this job for the same reason. He thinks Johnny Weeks is a danger to us all and that you're both cut from the same cloth. What do you say to that?'

'The problem with Jack is that he's a man with more than two faces,' I said.

Clements allowed himself a sharp, incredulous guffaw at my insubordination.

'He told me there's nothing wrong with arrogance,' I croaked.

'Good old Jack.'

Even with the guffaw Clements's concentration had remained entirely constant. He was ruthlessly pursuing his own agenda, moral or otherwise, and he wasn't about to let go of that.

'Everything is under control now, I know. Under your guidance Johnny is a reformed character . . .'

I nodded and shrugged at the same time. I didn't want any more than the minimum responsibility when it came to my charge. There was nothing reformed about Johnny.

'We love a reformed sinner,' Clements said. The *we* referred to the firm, but really, he was speaking personally. He was looking at me directly but referring to Johnny, of course.

Well why *of course*?

'We do,' I said.

Though his comment was so obviously loaded, there was something of his own humanity shining through. About the same measure as a tramp might glimpse when being given a bundle of Salvation Army hymn-books to sit on.

He began to talk about the firm. He was careful to tell me nothing I didn't already know, but he was selling me the principles by which it operated. It was as if he was grooming me for a managerial post. I nodded and grunted acknowledgements. Obviously he hadn't given much thought to the contents of my file if he had me marked for one of his future desktop analysts.

Presently, he glanced at his watch. He had to get back to the wedding party.

It was a credit to his manipulative skills that he had succeeded in creating the sense that we had all the time we wanted for our little talk, but now he was feeling the pressure of the clock. I also got the distinct impression that time was against him in a larger sense.

He had a way of making the tea go cold prematurely. Suddenly afternoon tea was over.

'By the way, Harry, has Jack Bradley made any' – and here there was just the slightest hesitation – 'special request of you lately? With regard to the operation, I mean.'

'No.' I replied cautiously. 'Nothing . . . out of the ordinary.' I wanted to ask what he meant by special, but of course I knew it would be pointless.

'Outline your instructions.'

I outlined my brief, such as it was.

'You will tell me if these instructions change, however slightly. You will report to me personally and speak to no one about it. Is that clear?'

'Yes.'

'You don't blab when you're drunk, do you, Harry?'

'I don't, sir.'

'Good man.'

He had already gathered up the cups and saucers.

'You want me to wash them?' I asked, standing up smartly. Getting to my feet quickly seemed to be important.

He didn't answer. He went into the kitchen with the tea things and returned promptly. His face betrayed that in the very short time he'd been away he had tested a threatening but unproven thesis and found his information wanting. On the way to meet Johnny for the first time Bradley had told me that there was no such thing as crisis, only opportunity. Evidently Clements didn't share Bradley's glib opinion.

'I should be with my family,' he said absently.

'Of course.' What was this? I hadn't taken him away. He had arranged the meeting. I moved towards the hall door. He followed, buttoning his formal jacket over his stomach.

'Don't use the mobile phone. Come directly to me.'

'I will, sir.'

'And how is your wife?' he asked, turning the key in the door behind us.

'I don't see her often, Mr Clements.'

He held back for a moment and stiffened his back to consider my position. 'Ah yes,' he said thoughtfully, and set off at a brisk pace.

'This fellow who's marrying my daughter . . . I'm not sure about him,' he confided. 'He's a member of Teddy Hall.' He pointed lamely over the roofs of the houses on the opposite side of the street, towards St Edmund Hall. 'Soon to be called to the Bar, he tells me. I had him checked. Not a thing on him. Nothing interesting. Nothing at all . . .'

He was trying to sound cheery; trying to smooth over our awkward interview.

'You don't like him, sir?' I might have been smirking.

'I don't, Harry, but that's not the point, is it?'

'I'm not the best one to ask, sir.'

'No. You're not. I've given them a damn good do.'

'I can see that.'

'Pity you can't come back with me to enjoy it.'

'I have to be on my way, sir.'

'Yes. You do, don't you.'

I stopped at the next street corner. 'I go up this way.'

He shook my hand. 'Remember,' he said in a paternal voice, 'I'm listening.'

He went on. In spite of the buzz of traffic and loud tourists that had gathered around me, I could hear the music from the wedding party wafting over an adjacent wall. I stood for a moment thinking about tin gods and Lollards.

CHAPTER 21

I didn't return to the car immediately. Instead, I wandered the streets. I thought George and his cigarette might be following me, but if he was I didn't see him. I walked as far as Magdalen Bridge and watched the punts on the muddy Cherwell. Oxford was all going to plan. It was providing Mr and Mrs Clements with the perfect day for their daughter's wedding, albeit to a twit, and Harry Fielding was alive and well and had a job with the firm protecting the realm from all harm. He could even take an hour off now to walk in the botanic gardens or pay a student to punt him up the river. He could take his time driving back to London. He had his mobile phone. They could contact him if he was needed urgently and he could put the boot down on the accelerator. Apprentice John was there to do his bidding, to do any donkey-work.

I walked quickly back up the High Street.

I left the busy car park, drove a short distance, turned down a narrow street that had a 'no through road' sign at its mouth. It had high walls on either side. Patches of evening light were climbing up the top half of one wall as the sun sank level with the rooftops of the city. There was a sharp bend leading to a closed wooden gate. I pulled the car up on to the scant strip of pavement to one side of the gate and switched off the engine.

Effectively a dog-leg cul-de-sac, it was a quiet place with little movement, save for the occasional pedestrian taking a short cut through an extension of the lane that ran at right angles under an arch behind me.

I sat there in the car a long time before setting off for London. I wanted to be sure I was sober, but really I needed to think in a quiet place. The bad feeling I had about the hostage job had surfaced and set alarm bells ringing as never before. Evidently, the rift between Clements and Bradley was deadly serious. The contention between the two men went far beyond office politics. I was having to nod in both directions just to save my own skin. The crux of it was the hostage-taking in order to flush out Target A.

Neither Clements nor Bradley was going to tell me anything that would enlighten me. Perhaps Bradley was fucking Clements's wife – now I was letting my own emotions interfere, and that was dangerous.

The job was moving to the next phase. Whatever was to happen at the safe house would happen soon. We would be briefed at short notice and do our duty and be damned.

I felt the weight of the automatic Bradley had issued me with. It fitted snugly into its underarm holster and the holster fitted not so snugly under my arm. What I thought about when I thought about me didn't include this lump under my arm. But that was vanity and this was an automatic that might one day soon be needed.

Any change of plan, however slight – wasn't that what Clements had said?

And on the other side of it, Johnny and I weren't to speak to anybody about these guns that Bradley had issued us. Nobody – wasn't that what Bradley had said? Did 'nobody' include Clements, and if it did, did that constitute a slight change of plan, that is, the plan Clements was referring to?

We'd have to get Apprentice John's crooked barrister friend from the nightclub to advise on the matter. What was meat and drink to a barrister could, in the long run, send people mad in the firm.

I was reversing the car, preparing to execute a three-point turn in the mouth of the arch, when the mobile phone rang. I answered. It was Johnny.

'I told you not to call me on this phone,' I said.

'It's Bradley. He's looking for us. He was trying to contact you.'

'I left the phone in the car.'

'Something is going down.' His voice was weighty, but I could tell he was excited. 'He's looking for us,' he repeated.

'Is he, now. Well, we'll be ready, won't we?'

Johnny correctly took it that he was not to ask where I was or how long it would be before we could rendezvous.

'Do we have a brief?' I asked.

'He wants us at the house. He'll call.'

'All right, then. What do you want? Curried chips, I suppose? I'm having a korma.'

'No-no. I'll have a korma, too.' He seemed surprised.

Some distance out of Oxford I took a turn off the main road and travelled down a lane to a large sloping field with a clump of trees at the bottom. There was a farmhouse on the rise so I rooted out the dirty old car rug that was in the boot and went for a walk into the trees.

I put most of the trees between me and the farm-house, then I stopped, took out the automatic from under my arm, released the safety catch, checked its cocking mechanism and ensured I had a full clip. I wrapped the car rug loosely around my gun hand to help muffle the sound. I expected that even without the muffling this model would make a relatively flat report in the countryside.

But I'm no expert, and this wasn't my choice of gun. I wanted to get a feel for it. I wanted to be reassured. I needed to do it while there was still some natural light.

I pointed it at a tree-trunk. Squeezed the trigger.

The hammer went to, but there was no contact. The bullet was not discharged.

I tried again.

The same.

Now this was where being no expert made me a little sick in the stomach.

I unwound the rug, examined the weapon, but could see nothing out of order. I tried a third time.

The same.

I drove over the speed limit most of the way back to London.

But I didn't stop there. I didn't go to our safe house. I came in on the M40 and passed the Hoover factory at a hell of a speed, then was forced to slow down by traffic. I made my way to Hyde Park, crossed the river by Vauxhall Bridge and headed towards Peckham, where I stopped to refuel and to make a phone call from a call-box. I rang a businessman and long-term associate who had retired to grow apples on his farm near Sittingbourne.

'Hello?'

'It's Harry.'

'Harry . . .' He sounded doubtful, but then he would, being security conscious.

'Harry Fielding.'

'Ah yes. And how are you?'

'I'm well, but I have a problem.'

'Well, Harry, I'm watching the boxing on the telly.' His voice sounded a little weaker than I remembered.

'I need to see you.'

'No. You don't need to see me. I tell you what, Harry, next time I'm up in London we'll have a drink in the French House. What do you say? Give me a number. I'll give you a call.'

'Look, I'm sorry. This isn't the usual request.'

'Doesn't matter. I'm finished.'

'I need just five minutes of your time.'

'I'll be up in London soon. We'll have a long chat.'

'I need to see you tonight. I'll meet you anywhere you say.'

'I've nothing for you.'

'You can help me. You can set my mind at ease.'

There was a brief silence at the other end. I was running out of coins.

'You come here. Don't call before the boxing is over, there's a good chap.'

The line went dead.

I got back into the car and drove to Blackheath and

on towards Kent. There wasn't a big fight on that night. Perhaps they were showing a few bouts on the general sports round-up.

When I say businessman, I mean he had been a gunsmith and discreet supplier of small arms.

Some two hours later I pulled up to his house along a lane lined with hops on one side and apple trees on the other. I had been lost for a time having taken the wrong exit from the M2.

He had been watching for me, because the car head-lights had scarcely swept across the face of the house before the hall door was opened and he was out to meet me. I took it that he didn't want me in the house. And I was right. He put his hand out for me to shake.

'Harry Fielding, you're looking well,' he boomed. Freddie could be boorish but I had always seen through that.

I shook his hand firmly. The firmness was in antici-pation of his heavy one-stroke action, which I always imagined was the greeting I would get were I to meet a nuclear physicist who was going to show me his bomb. Were Freddie showing you the bomb you could be sure it was the real thing, and the viewing would be discreet.

'Thanks. And I want to stay well.'

'Walk?'

'All right.'

There was a bright moon in a clear sky. That was why it was cold. We went walking on a clay path through his orchard. He had come prepared. He was wearing a heavy jacket, from the pockets of which he produced a hip-flask.

'Want some?'

I didn't particularly want spirits, but I took a swig.

'What do you want?'

I didn't waste any time. I produced the automatic.

'I want you to look at this.'

He took it from me, turned it over in his hands, worked the cocking mechanism, checked the clip.

'You wouldn't have got this from me.'

'You like that model?'

He took a swig from the flask. 'A bit noisy by itself.'

By itself meant without a silencer.

'Reliable?'

He shrugged. 'Has been known to jam.' He was never one to impress with technical jargon or comprehensive detail.

'It's not working.'

'I know.'

'You can tell just by looking at it?'

'I know it's not working because you've come from London to show it me.'

He offered me another swig. Which I took.

He put me with my gun in a storage barn that had a heady smell of sour and rotting apples.

'You see that table there,' he said, pointing to a rough board table that was cluttered with tools and scrap, 'clear that, will you?'

He left for the house, and I had just set to work when my mobile phone rang. It was Bradley.

'Where are you?'

'I'm on my way to the house.'

'Where are you?'

'I'm helping a friend with a problem.' I could tell he was sitting on his rage. With operational matters you just can't lie about your availability. 'It will take me two hours to get to the house.'

'I need you in the house with Weeks. You may have compromised the entire operation.'

'I'll be there in two hours, Jack.'

'Don't *Jack* me. I'll call you with the brief.'

The line went dead immediately.

My friend returned with a small kit and something wrapped in velvet. He unwrapped the velvet as though he had Napoleon's penis to show me. In fact, it was a silencer that fitted the automatic.

'I wasn't sure I still had this.'

He screwed it on to the barrel of my gun, cocked it, pointed out the open door, and fired.

Nothing. No bullet discharged.

He took a magnifying glass out of his kit and examined the weapon.

'It's been tampered with, all right,' he said. 'And a good job they've done.'

He showed me where the hammer had been filed, but I still couldn't see it for myself.

'Thanks, Freddie.'

There wasn't a question of money changing hands. If you can get a service like that, you don't pay for it.

Under the circumstances you would have expected him to shake my hand, advise me to be extra careful, and wish me good luck. But Freddie really was retired and his silence on the matter was his way of asserting that fact.

'Looking forward to seeing you in London, then,' he said. He didn't shake my hand. Instead, he gave me another automatic, similar to the one I was leaving behind. 'That's the best I can do.'

It had taken him some twenty minutes to retrieve it from its hiding place.

I didn't leave my number and he didn't expect me to do so. There was just the slightest chance we would run into each other and have that drink in the French House, but it would have to be left to fate. I knew that if I rang and invited him he would always be busy with his family or with his apples.

Besides the blackness of the night and the cutting diamond headlights swiping past me, I remember two things about the drive back to London. One was another phone call from Johnny. The other was the second call from Jack Bradley.

Chapter 22

I sat in the car at the end of the street, out of sight of the windows of the house. I was thinking very hard about driving away. Going to ground. I had done it before. I'm good at that. It would be straightforward. I would be safe.

Johnny was in the house by himself with the hostage, being deadly efficient, not panicking. All right, so you didn't ever want to have Johnny guarding you if you were unfortunate enough to be a hostage, but he had learned some self-control since we started. The tape on the hostage's mouth would be overdone, and the cuffs a little tight on his wrists, but Johnny would be hunched in a corner of the room on the first floor, watching over his charge. Johnny would have established his infidel monster credentials by eye contact alone.

Johnny and I would speak later and I would educate him further and he, too, would run to safety. He was sure to have more than the one Spanish hideaway.

This clandestine action was unofficial in the extreme. The firm could not be seen to be responsible. Johnny and I were what we had been at the outset – understrappers.

I was about to turn the key in the ignition when I saw a car slow as it passed the house. It came around the block a second time. I got a closer look at the occupants.

They pulled up across the street from me. It was my worst fears realised. I had seen their type before. Seen them in London. Seen some of their handiwork. Moscow gangsters. Ex-Special Forces. The Russian capital was full of these guys. Half of them working as criminals, the other half working for the police. Ex-comrades shooting at each other over cases of killer vodka, illegal arms and drugs. Some shooting straight, more shooting wide.

The assassination business is syndicated. The jobs are passed down through a network, with the thug at the end of the food chain pulling the trigger for just a few hundred dollars.

The ones operating in London, whether temporarily resident or just paying a quick visit, were somewhat more exotic than the lowest form of gangster life. They tended to be the ones who, until recently, had been working for the police and had been fired or had changed their minds. They're the straight-shooting type.

Whichever kind, they like their silenced automatic weapons. No such thing as overkill. Some are more stealthy than others, but when it comes to the shooting itself there is invariably a ham-fisted thoroughness that sometimes stretches to a good kicking after the bullets have been discharged.

It's as if they have been told that a body has six pints of blood and all of it has to be drained. The ham-fistedness extends to that brand of sentimentality.

I saw them make ready with their packages. They

were taking their time. My head said turn the key in the ignition, but my hand reached for the door lever.

I thought of entering via the basement, but decided I would be too easily spotted. I went around the back. Up one drainpipe on to the slanting roof of the return, then up a second pipe to the main roof, and in via a skylight. It was the route I had chosen on my first reconnaissance of the house for Bradley's little game, but it seemed so much more difficult this time.

I came down the stairs slowly behind the automatic. I had to be extra light on my feet because of the bare stairboards. I do not have lightning reactions with a pistol but I have a steady hand and I go for the sure shot.

This was not reassuring as I descended the staircase.

Where were my dead friends now? Not one around to do some bullet-catching. I was thinking about our man in the suit being too tall and not ducking in time. I was only an inch or two shorter. These thoughts came floating out of my head. Out of the dream box, it seemed, for this descent of the stairs had an air of unreality to it. I had a strong urge to call out Johnny's name. To warn him and to run.

Remember, Johnny, I wanted to say, I have to take my time with a gun – and these are professional assassins. But then I thought about Johnny's lousy shooting. I couldn't see him stabbing them both in the chest with his Teddy boy's flick-knife before they blew the back of his head out.

I checked again to make sure the safety catch was disengaged.

Then I thought I might be able to get him and the hostage out before they came.

Then I saw them coming up the stairs. I was surprised by the amount of noise they made.

Johnny, don't you hear them coming?

Johnny, you're not listening.

Johnny, they're at the bend in the stairs below me.

'Harry,' I heard Johnny call, and I heard his footfalls as he advanced to the door. I saw the killers make ready as they advanced. They had their guns aimed when he opened the door.

I caught the first one on the crown of the head with my first shot. His head went down through the floor, I thought.

The second one swung, canted his MAC machine-gun and fired in an instant. Little splinters of plaster blasted my ear as I dropped. Johnny must have levelled his pistol at this one because I heard two flat clicks from the disabled gun.

This is it, boy, the little voice said, two shots in rapid succession because he's sweeping back and won't miss.

I heard Johnny roar as the second burst of automatic fire came from the machine-gun. He must have had the knife out by now.

I discharged most of the clip. The second shot hit high in the chest. Johnny plunged the long, narrow blade into his neck.

I sat down on the stairs and shook the plaster out of my ear.

Johnny pulled the blade out. He still had the defective pistol in his right hand. He pointed it at the assassin's head, squeezed the trigger.

Another flat click. He looked at it incredulously, like a schoolboy asking who had ever heard of a gun that didn't shoot?

Then, he looked to me. The smell of cordite curled up into my nostrils. Johnny had already turned the knife around in his hand ready for a downward stabbing stroke if needed.

I got us both out of there quickly. We abandoned the bound, gagged and drugged hostage who was tied to my bed. We hurried down the stairs and left by the front door.

I gave Johnny my old address and told him to drive us there. I was shaking. I gave him an explanation of sorts as we drove to my ex-wife. It was more than a dog should have to take in.

Bradley, I explained, wanted to undermine Clements's operation. He wanted to force the issue of pre-emptive covert work, and show that the head of the Service wasn't up to it. Bradley was for intervention, remember, Johnny?

Johnny remembered.

A disastrous operation would play right into Bradley's hands. The Lollards would have their way in the new offensive on international terrorism. Johnny and I were trouble. We were expendable. There would still be a hell of a fuss over a botched operation of this magnitude, and, of course, Bradley would make sure that the unofficial brief would be seen to have come from Clements personally. The Joint Intelligence Committee would judge harshly. Clements would be discredited. Bradley would get his Bodleian chair.

This action had blown apart the veils of enmity

between Clements and Bradley to reveal a stark reality. Policy differences and office politics had brought about crude action with hard consequences. For Johnny and me ramifications didn't come any bigger, short of the assassins having succeeded.

I told Johnny about our defective guns. Bradley didn't want us being better than the opposition. Better to have the bodies of two agents along with one dead hostage. The attack would be blamed on Target A's old enemies.

Johnny just kept looking back at me.

I wanted to see my wife before I went to ground. I wanted to tell her that I loved her and to beg her not to believe anything Bradley might say about me.

Johnny waited in the car. I went to the door. She answered and I pushed past into the hall.

'What are you doing here at this time of night?' she demanded.

I tried to speak but the words wouldn't pass my throat. Instead, they slid back down and dissolved in a sour mess in my stomach.

I took a firm hold of her.

'Harry. Let go. What's the matter? Harry, you're hurting me.'

I pushed her away. I pushed her with undue force. She fell at the foot of the stairs. That was when Bradley came at me with a knife. He must have come from the kitchen. I didn't see him until he was right on top of me.

He didn't know to twist it or to pull it up. He couldn't make a second stab. I pulled out the automatic and pressed the barrel of the gun to his forehead. I could see him thinking now about a second lunge with the knife. Perhaps he was thinking that he was safe with the defective gun.

I glanced at my wife. She was getting to her feet by moving backwards up the stairs on the heels of her hands. She was in shock, but she was shaking her head.

Jack Bradley had nothing to say to me. He was sure he still had the upper hand.

I glanced again at my wife. Slowly, I moved the gun away from Bradley's head. There was a white oval in the middle of his forehead from the pressure of the barrel.

'On your way, Harry,' he said in a cracked voice.

Because of her shaking her head I didn't do it. I looked at her one last time. She was staring at the blood that was coming out of the small of my back.

I didn't squeeze the trigger. I took a few paces backwards. I was a god. I could have gone upstairs and cleaned my teeth with her toothbrush and wept.

There were no explanations. I turned and walked away.

CHAPTER 23

I had persuaded Johnny to leave me at the hospital. It made sense that we split up. I gave him the automatic, sent him on his way and went looking for a vacant bed. I didn't want to go to the Casualty department. I didn't want to be sedated. I wanted to think. I wanted to sleep for just a short time. If I could just close my eyes, I thought. If I could cram my ears with something warm and wet. If I could do that I could sleep. If I could sleep I might stop trying to measure one man's suffering against another's well-being. I might feel whole again.

I looked at all the sick people as I passed. I found a vacant bed on the third floor. I tried to shut my eyes but they sprang open again. It was scarcely a blink. I had tried to reason myself to sleep. In the past this had been a mechanism of great reliability.

'You're good in a tight spot,' I heard Juno say. 'Always have been.'

You want to take a statement like that from your ex-wife as a compliment. But her words dredged up in me a profound sadness. I could think of nothing to say in response. The skill that got me out of tight spots had left me dumb. It had left me with my eyes open. What could I say to her that didn't exclude her? I could look at my watch. I could tell her the time. They were handing round cups of tea. And that seemed an extraordinary proposition to me. I could hear the trolley coming up the corridor. The trolley burst through the double doors on the end of a pair of very long arms. The kitchen porter attached to the arms was an exceptionally tall man with sloping shoulders and a thatch of poodle hair that was on crooked. He wasn't expecting the bed to be occupied but he wasn't surprised to see me lying there looking very ill.

He glanced at the six patients in the eight-bed ward. They hadn't been expecting me either, but they sent no meaningful signals back to him. In a hospital you don't ask what a sick person is doing lying down on a bed.

Where were my pyjamas? Was that what he was thinking? I should have been in my pyjamas. Go on, ask me.

He didn't ask. Instead, he offered me tea and asked if I was going home.

'Yes,' I replied. 'Going home.'

'Tea?'

'Yes. I'm thirsty. Very thirsty.'

Weak tea in a white cup. There was also cake. Swiss roll put on a plate with a pair of tongs, and bread and jam. I had never seen jam as red as this. Was I dying?

'It'll be nice to get home,' he said.

Did he see the chart at the end of the bed was blank? His smile told me he would bring me a mountain of Swiss roll and a reservoir of tea if I showed a bit of fight.

'I said, it'll be lovely to get home,' he repeated.

'Yes, it will . . .'

His head went to one side and his smile gradually disappeared. That alerted me to the blood seeping through the bandage I had put on. It was seeping

274

out on to the bed cover beneath the small of my back.

'Good man' he said. 'You want more tea you tell me.'

'Yes, I will.'

I thought he was moving on to serve the others, but he just pushed his trolley a little further into the room, then left. I knew he was going to the nurses' station.

Move, I told my body. I used my calm, reassuring voice.

Nothing happened.

I would count to three.

One, two, three.

I couldn't get up.

I tried again. I took my time counting to three.

I'm asleep with my eyes open, I decided. Harry, I said, you're not always right in the head when you sleep. I had broken my wife's nose in my sleep. In my unconscious state my fist had swung down on her face. She's had a little bump on her nose ever since.

Three – and wake. Start with the legs. Swing those legs across, get those feet down on the floor.

I could hear footsteps. They were louder than they should have been. Was that because they were Juno's? My mind was racing, but without traction. They'll have to hose me out of here, I was thinking.

There was a stethoscope over by the sink. Which doctor had left it there? Didn't they know they were not meant to leave those down just anywhere? They could be used for listening at windows.

Was that my wife shouting down the hospital corridor – Harry Fielding, formerly my life partner, the man who forgets nothing and learns nothing? Never mind Bradley, had she got rid of the awful sheepskin rug in the bedroom? She paid three hundred and fifty pounds for it. You can buy a whole, live sheep for thirty quid. Juno, let me kiss the bump on your nose.

If I died before she reached the bed would she know that the dead miss the living more than the living miss the dead?

In her absence I couldn't get a picture of her. Couldn't fix her in my mind, and that was no good for a man putting things right.

The footfalls got louder, but the doors opened gently. It wasn't her. It was Johnny. He had decided to come back. He smiled and calmly gave an affirmative nod, as though making a normal hospital visit. Still too much of a dog, but he was learning his craft.

'There you are, Harry. Nobody could tell me where they put you.'

He could see the blood on the bed cover. I could see him trying to make some quick decisions about moving me. I think I might have called him Juno, but it didn't matter. I knew there wasn't much time.

He jangled his set of car keys. 'I'm double-parked.'

I reached out an arm and he came to assist me.

And suddenly, there we were – the two of us shuffling along the pavement, a katabatic wind at our backs. One of us bursting with desire and expectation – that was me, the one with the stab wound; the other relying too much on chance – that was him, the one with the pistol I had given him under his belt, the pistol with one bullet in it.

The Apprentice John I had come to know would

always take his chances, and right now that was all that mattered.

And where were we going with my knife wound and his one bullet? To his hideaway in Spain, perhaps, where we would sit under a carob-tree and drink red wine with ice in it, Johnny insisting on doing his waiter thing while others hunted the man with the suitcase bomb.

He whispered words of encouragement, but I didn't catch them in the first instance, so he repeated them.

'Look at me, Harry. This way. We're making all the right moves. Look at me.'

'I'm looking,' I said, but I wasn't. Nor did I feel the need to whisper. If I had turned to look at him I think I would have fallen down. I tried to take him in with my peripheral vision, but he was too close. It must have been his hand that was holding my arm. Now, how long had he been doing that?

The pain was coming. I tried not to concentrate on it. I tried to expel a bad taste by breathing through my mouth. Look at that woman, I instructed myself, the one directly in our path. She's looking hard at you. She thinks you're smiling at her with your mouth open.

She was the skinniest woman I had ever seen. I could have slid her into the slit in my back. As she passed she turned her hard look on Johnny. He returned a fake, lecherous leer to deflect her gaze.

At some point during one of our long Druid nights he told me that he had deposited sperm in a sperm bank. In the event of his death, he said, the contents of the frozen phial were to be given to the woman he called his girlfriend.

But that was just talk. Just fantasy. That Johnny loved

this woman, there was no doubt. He was sure he was invincible on the days he was with her. Did he know that love does not keep you from harm?

In the end a man is forced to act. And most of the action, I was thinking, was to do with recovering that which has been lost.

You think these thoughts, and then something else happens.

I wasn't looking to join absent friends. I wasn't anxious to catch up. I hadn't decided who I wanted to take me across to the other side – John Lennon, my old friend Alfie, or even the old man. I had made a better job of dying just calling to my wife's house to tell her we should get back together.

The dead – who knows what they are at, or how they have changed? It was a dead man who put that to me, and I had had the good sense to ignore the question.

I was in the immediate and present moment and Johnny was looking out for us. In spite of my stupid body movements I was sure the wind could not knock me to the ground.

The notion of invicibility had a powerful effect. This bleeding was going to stop. The scar would bake in the sun. I was going to live to feel the blood slowing in my veins, slowing as it does with age, and with any kind of contentment.

I could see Apprentice John and Tina in the back seat of his almost bulletproof car somewhere in a parched landscape, him finally and properly inside her.

I, of course, was not there. I was somewhere else. No knife wound. No private bleeding. Very much alive and on my way.